Hardcastle Classics Presents

JUST LOVE ENOUGH

A London Hustle Book

WILL FORREST

JUST LOVE ENOUGH

2ND EDITION

Cover & book design by Hardcastle Books

Images licenced from Depositphotos

www.hardcastlebooks.com

ISBN: 978-1-990115-89-9

10 9 8 7 6 5 4 3 2 1

JUST LOVE ENOUGH

for AHF

It was the best of jobs, it was the worst of jobs, it was the age of liberty, it was the age of dirty secrets, it was the epoch of glorious progress, it was the same old story it always is, of a boy without prospects, born at the bottom, with no notion of how to get up.

So when a chance came round, I grabbed it, and you can't tell me you'd not have done the same if you'd had my life to live. That was the only way I'd ever got anything, by grabbing it, scant enough food on our table that it was always a race. A knock-down, drag 'em out, knuckles and knees and teeth kind of race, which is what one gets with five elder brothers in a one-room flat and a Pa who can't keep a job for the sickness and a Ma who can only make porridge and salt-fat stretch so far.

How I got the job is its own tale, and if we end up sitting here long enough I'll tell it to you. The job itself is what interests most people.

HONEST WORK

It was honest work and that was good enough. A thought which sustained Noel daily, through scorching sun and pelting rain, through grey weeks when the plants seemed to weep for want of light, and sudden frosts that crushed a year's ambitions in the span of an evening. Tallying his losses, he could reflect that he'd yet to succumb to The Life, let his surroundings and the truth of his prospects overcome his morals. *Thou Shalt Not Steal*: one couldn't get much clearer about an instruction than having the Almighty carve it in stone, then enforce it with eternal damnation.

The proof was all around him, for hadn't his old mate Mick Raleigh gone and got himself sent up just last week for that upper story job at that lord's house in Surrey? Other childhood friends had met a similar fate or worse, like poor Willis who'd fallen from his father's dray last summer and broken his head open on the paving stones, proving that one didn't need to do wrong to go wrong.

Still, Noel longed for the feeling of clean skin, for the dirt never went away, no matter how hard he scrubbed his hands and arms, his neck, his face, his clothes. Good, honest dirt, in his fingernails and ears and between his teeth so that every mouthful of food grated. Dirt bursting from the nap of his hair in a silty cloud whenever he touched his head, put on a hat, laid his head on his pillow. Dirt forever, as between the efforts of him and his parents and his two sisters, they barely made do on the earnings from their garden allotment on the northeast edge of London.

That Noel ever had brass in pocket was only on account of the hemp tobacco he pushed round sailors' pubs and to Old Agnes, whom everyone called a witch for no reason except she was cross-eyed and ugly and sold tinctures to housemaids... Fine. He was a witch's apothecary and a pusher and a dirt-covered tenant farmer, and it might as well have been a thousand years ago and himself a serf for all the dignity his labour gained him.

Except a thousand years ago he'd have been a spear-tossing tribesman with as little notion of what was to become of England as the bleeding English had. Two hundred years ago, he'd have been worse than a serf. A hundred years, he would be his great-great-grandfather, driving the buggy round his owner's sugar plantation on the hill above Montego Bay. At fifty years, his grandfather, unacknowledged in his master's will despite all his promises to reward him for such devoted personal service, then sold off with the chattels of the estate. The rest of the story Noel knew from having lived it.

But the night was clear and the moon was rising and he was at his leisure till morning. After locking the shed he ambled towards the river through the beds of the other allotment-holders. Soon enough Dame Progress would catch up with them, plough under the tidy rows of beans and potatoes for factory workers' homes. The riverbank had been shored up with bricks and rocks and bits of paving stone to form a causeway from the gardens to the stub of a dock, something to keep barrow wheels and boots from sinking into the mud. Noel had nailed together a bench from odd planks, a place to sit that wasn't the dirty ground. He sat with care, minding the creaks, the sagging back board, but the repairs could wait.

He got out some tobacco and twisted a pinch into a paper. Mum would clout him good, which is why he did this here, and not too often or he'd get a taste for it. No, it was just now and then that one ought to indulge in any given pleasure. He exhaled slowly, a thin stream that blurred the stars and their reflection in the oily blackness of the river.

"That's a filthy habit," someone said. A slender bloke in a swell suit was coming down through the gardens. Noel was about to issue a challenge for trespass when the man took off his hat and Izzy Pound's curls sprung up.

"Cobber! When'd you get out?" Noel asked, standing to shake hands, Izzy's pale skin as smooth as if it was gloved.

"Get out of what?"

"The poke. That's where I expect shits like you to be when I ain't seen them in months."

"I weren't in prison."

"That's obvious now that I've had a butcher's." Those really were gloves. Izzy was turned out proper, from his new boots on up. Clothes made to fit, not some chop job of his elder brothers' or a cloth copy of a better suit, but tailored gabardine in a tight grey check. The bulge of a watch in his pocket. The smell of women about him, a mix of perfume, hair tonic, and sex. "It's grand to see you, Iz. I was sure you'd got sent."

He smiled, the same crooked grin as always. "Still might happen."

"Who's it you're working for?"

"No one we know. And it's not like you think."

"You're not in the Life?"

"No. Lord no. Not that one at any rate."

"Yet you've the brass for this get up? You're holding out on me, Pound. I ain't laid eyes on you for months. Now you swan up dressed like a nob, telling porkies about some job. If you got a job, how'd you get off?"

"How'd I what? I mean, I'm on leave a few nights. Boss's orders. Overwork, she said."

"She? Never mind, it's grand to see you, Iz." Noel sat again, leaving space beside for Izzy to join him. The last year had changed his friend's face, carved away the softness of youth, sharpened his profile, made him properly handsome. "What's brought you all the way out here?" he asked.

"I'm at a bit of a loose end," Izzy replied, rubbing his neck. "All I been doing these days is work. I forgot how I used to put in time."

"Come to Mum's. She'll give you a feed."

His old friend chuckled wryly. "I better not."

"Well, now you gotta tell me who you're working for. It's not Muldoon?"

"I bleeding hope not."

"You don't know?"

"You can't be sure sometimes who owns what. But she would have said..."

"Who would?"

"I ought not to say."

"Not a chance, Pound. If you're getting as good as what got you all this, I might want to get in myself."

"You what? I mean...shit." Izzy stood abruptly. Backed away. "Forget I said anything, all right? I ought to leave you be."

"Don't go, man. Are you in trouble?"

"No."

"Is it bad?"

"I'm not mixed up in anything."

"Then tell me. Whatever your secret is, it's eating you up. And we been friends long enough, cobber. Who am I to judge?"

"All right, but you gotta swear this never goes beyond the two of us."

"Of course."

Izzy had come over all intense, eyes gleaming, jaw set. "Swear."

"All right, I swear not to breathe a word of what you tell me to another living soul. Now, have a pull of this and settle yourself." Noel lit the sailor's twist and passed it to Izzy, who held it as clumsily as ever, like it was some French harlot's cigarette, though at least he'd learned how not to cough.

"Cor, that's something," he wheezed as he handed it back.

"Innit? Now sit your nobby arse back down and spill

your guts."

HOUSE OF LORDS

"MIND THAT IF YOU'D told me a year ago that this was what's coming I'd have called you a bull-shitter of the highest order. Back then I was scraping a few shillings a week out of rough jobs, mucking out horses and digging holes. All my wages went to the family. Da was down with the gout again, his toes swelled like purple eggs. Then Matthew took sick and couldn't work, Pete had fucked off again, me and Luke were carrying the rest of them, and it was growing less possible by the day.

For a change I was clean the day I met Ursula. Had gone to the jobbers' as I ever did but had been passed over, weary of most offers (digging graves, digging sewers, digging in general) and too slow to claim the better (stirring glue, hauling coal.) Noon came and I was still unemployed, and by habit found myself strolling towards the House.

If it's meant to be a secret, the high-toned bawdy called The House of Lords is a bloody great blaring secret decorated with bunting and fronted by a band. It's practically a funding arm of the police force between bribes and free trade for the bobbies. Ma had told me off heaps for hanging round Spencer Street, but those women were hard to ignore, blazing like stars, trailing fragrance and glamour as they came and went from their place of employ. My even being in that part of town was a bit of a dare, an idle youth in a sacking jacket and flap-toed shoes amid the tailored suits and top hats, the swishy silks and buttoned boots.

I was passing the door I'd seen the clients use when a woman appeared on the footpath ahead. As if from thin air, stepping out from behind an ad hoarding that half blocked the mouth of an alley. She was dressed in swagged black silk, her bolero lapelled like a dinner jacket, beneath this a snow-white shirt buttoned up to her chin, her hat like a gentleman's Trilby, though she wore it as ladies do, perched high on the front of her blonde hair and trimmed with ribbon. Rather than a parasol she had a walking stick. As she crossed Spencer and headed on her way, a man you and I know very well stepped away from the opposite corner and followed her.

Like the gormless moppet I most surely am, I went after them. At first to be sure Joycey was after her. And then, once he'd ran a few paces to keep her in sight, to decide if my life was worth spending on saving a woman I was quite sure was a whore.

Joycey wanted something, perhaps not her but the little leather purse tucked under her arm. Whatever his aim, he'd treat her brutally in the taking. And there I was, a foot shorter and at most half Joycey's weight, wracking my brain for the quickest, easiest way to disable him without getting my neck broke.

"ALL RIGHT, ALL RIGHT, lemme stop you right there," Noel said. "You did not bloody well do down Michael Joycey in broad flipping daylight."

"Too right I didn't. But I couldn't stand by and do nothing. She hadn't done nothing to deserve it. Just making a living, and a hard one too, and Joycey was going to pluck it from her hands and likely molest her while he was about it. Or at least that's what I thought was gonna happen."

"She fought him?"

Izzy laughed aloud. "Cobber, she near blinded him. If there's something that woman knows, it's how to hurt a man."

"But Joycey?"

"I only saw the end. Got stuck behind some old biddies in their shawls. When I dodged around, she'd turned up another street. He'd gone after, and I went after him, caught sight of him shoving her into an alley."

"The cheek!"

"I got there right as she was bashing him across the chops with her cane."

"What's a bash to the chops to Joycey?"

"A lot when it's done with a lump of pewter shaped like a raven's beak. I mean, it weren't the cleanest hit. He'd come up behind her and got his arm round her waist to grab that little purse of hers, as she keeps it chained onto herself. I think he'd meant to get his other hand round her throat. But she wasn't having a bar of it. Just kept swinging the stick." Izzy waved an arm in imitation, striking at invisible devils on his back.

"That must have been a sight."

"It was horrible, to be fair. She must have stunned him with the first hit, cause she landed a good few more before he had the sense to let go. Blood all over him." Shuddering, Izzy spat to one side. The ebbing tide had bared the mud at the riverbanks, raising the inevitable stench which came towards them in a wave as a heavy barge beat up the middle channel, stirring the silty water. Izzy covered his nose. "Blow me, I forgot how it stinks down here."

"You're getting soft, Pound." Noel prodded his chum in the gut, striking more muscle than expected.

"That I am. And famished. Come on, I'll shout you a perpendicular at the Lion's Head."

"But you ain't done your tale, are you?"

"Me? I'm just getting started."

Joycey had knocked her hat off so I grabbed it and went after. She'd won, but she was at least a little hurt, limping and leaning on the cane, and I caught up quick. Offered her back her hat.

"I would have helped you," I told her, like an absolute berk, which was pretty much how she looked at me as she put on the hat.

"You still might have a chance to be useful. Why don't you escort me? You can keep an eye out for any of Mr Joycey's associates." Her voice had a toothiness to it, something foreign, something mighty compelling. She was terribly pretty as well, with that purity of face that makes men surrender without a second thought.

"Tell me why you followed me," she said once we were walking.

"I didn't mean no harm. It's just...I know who you are."

"Do you?"

"You're one of the women. From that house," I added when she looked at me odd.

"One of the women? What does that mean?"

"I'd rather not say in public, like."

"If you did you'd be wrong."

"But didn't I see you come out that alley? By that place everyone calls The House of Lords. The bawdy house," I added in a whisper.

"Perhaps you did, but I'm not one of the women. I'm the proprietress."

"You run it?"

"I own it."

"Golly!"

"Yes, that's often the response. Here we are." We'd stopped in front of a grey office building in a row of similar, each with its little plaque stuck beside the door.

"Ought I to wait for you?"

She looked me over once again, a flick of the eye up and down. "If you wish."

With that she went in, and it was like waking up. I suddenly cottoned to where I was, deep in Westminster, intending to loiter in front of some solicitor's office as if I had any right to be there.

Which of course I went right ahead and did. Of course not standing there, but pacing up one side of the street and down the other, pausing to read the bills posted up on the pillars, biding time as one does. Joycey himself couldn't have cased it more discretely. As to why, murphy knows. For no reason beyond curiosity I had followed this woman halfway across town and thought to fight a man I'd seen do genuine murder. So what was a bit of bother from the rozzers for loitering? But the lady came out again quick and off we went.

"What's your name?" she asked.

"Pound. Ezekiel Pound, ma'am. Though they call me Izzy."

"Have you been in school?"

"I can read, if that's what you're asking."

"Are you employed?"

"If I was, would I have been loafing around your doorway?"

"I'm in need of a young man."

"Hey, now—"

"Not as trade. I've another shop in Haymarket in need of a runner. Someone with a sharp eye and a closed mouth."

"And where might this runner be going that he has to run to get there?"

"All manner of places. In part, we need a lookout. The constabulary have been paying rather arbitrary visits to Mrs Owen, and it is badly complicating our operations."

"Say that in plain English, if you don't mind."

"You're to spy on the beat police and tell Owen when they're coming so she can warn the custom to pull up their trousers and get out."

"Is that all?"

"She'll need you for other errands. And a male presence will lend a bit of authority."

"I'm hardly a male presence, to be fair."

"I'll pay you two shillings a day."

"When can I start?"

WHAT A MAN CAN LOSE

"So that was me for a good six months. Runner wasn't a joke, and I reckon by now there's not a laneway in Haymarket I don't know by heart." Izzy speared the last bit of chop and smeared it through the drippings on his plate before eating it.

"But you ain't working there now, are you?"

"Nah. I got promoted. She popped me in this real fizzing get-up. Black tails, scarlet benjy, a haircut and all. Had me serving drinks. That went on for a couple more months." The barkeep was near and Izzy waved for another pair of pints. Noel's head was already singing, not aided by the volume of the public house, which had filled during the course of their counter meal. They took their beers and moved off to where the crowd was thinner, by the door which let in puffs of damp evening air with every swing.

Noel set his glass on the plaster window sill to twist up another pinch of tobacco and wait for Izzy to go on, but his friend had lapsed into reflection, watching the ebb and flow of men over the edge of his glass. His suit was even finer in the light, so much that Noel had cringed to see him lean his elbows on the greasy bar. It was still Izzy Pound in the suit, though there was more of him than before, his frame filled out as if he ate this well all the time, no longer that hunted look about him, like a rat who knew that at the mouth of the hole waited a trap.

If he didn't know him Noel might have took him for a proper gentleman, at least middle class, some banker's son about his leisure of a springtime eve. The rorty little bugger had even buffed his fingernails. Noel's hands were so permanently soiled he'd marked up the cigarette paper, only the pink of his palms to confirm that he was seeing his own skin and not more dirt.

"Come on, Pound, finish your story," he said. "You've got me hanging."

"I wot? I mean, right. Well, there's not much to tell from there." Izzy took a long pull on his pint, still watching the room. Noel exhaled across his face, making him blink. "What the fuck, Peters?"

"Not much to tell, my black arse. You're holding out, Pound."

"I wot?"

"Look at you. That ain't the dunnage of a man on two shilling a day. Even twice that."

Izzy's face was turning pinker by the second. He took another gulp of beer then turned to Noel, eyes bright. "You cannot tell a soul. Not a bleeding word of this to anyone."

"You know I'm no grasser."

Izzy shut his eyes, swallowed like he'd been fed bitter

medicine. He exhaled a shaky breath then leaned even closer, speaking soft and swiftly. "I went on a few months, right? And then this one chap...well, he offered me an awful lot of money. And so I went to Ursula and asked what she thought I ought to do."

"And she sold your lilywhite without a thought, didn't she?"

"Nah, that's not her way. Not at all."

"You didn't take him up on it, did you? *Did you*? Fucking hell, Pound..."

"I know, I know," he murmured into his glass, his eyes darting about the cramped room. "But you can't breathe a word of this."

"Who'd bloody well believe me?"

"I wouldn't have, a year ago."

"So that's your job?"

Izzy nodded, lips pressed tight, trapped by his confession.

"So how much are you earning of an evening?"

He didn't reply out loud, instead flashed their old hand sign for three, holding his fingers behind his glass like they were counting cards.

"Shillings?" Izzy shook his head slightly. "Crowns? Not bleeding pounds..."

"On average. I get a gratuity here and there."

"You fucker." The word burst from Noel's lips. Izzy laughed and took a drink of his lager, while Noel gaped at him like he'd sprouted a second head. "You absolute... Like, I'm not missing your essential point, am I?"

"I don't expect so."

"Like you *work* at that house."

"I do."

Noel had to stop and swallow the drool puddling on his tongue. Such a sum... The economics were staggering when set beside the effort he'd need to expend to earn as much. He looked at his hand clutching his glass, his nails rimmed with dirt, knuckles scraped raw from scrubbing and the hours of labour preceding. "How...how...how ugly are they?" he heard himself ask. "I mean, on average?"

"The custom? I dunno, average ugly. I don't spend much time gazing affectionately into their eyes, know what I mean?"

"No, but... Fucking hell, Pound."

"I know. Not at all what I thought I'd be doing to earn a crust."

"But you do it."

"I do."

In a month, he'd have paid out his debts. In six months, his parents.' In a year or two, he'd have a house bought. All he had to do was let an untold number of men... "Fucking hell, Pound."

"You're the only one who knows."

"I ain't saying boo." They went on without speaking, the noise of the pub barely reaching Noel's ears, as if they'd stepped into another room. Indeed it was like having gone to a new place, a sweetly scented world without dirt or stooping or the humiliation of bartering with bargemen over a ha'penny worth of carrots, begrudging each ha'penny lost. He went to drink; the glass was empty, and he put it on the windowsill, where it promptly tipped and rolled off. Izzy caught it easily in one hand.

"Noel, cobber, you look a bit green round the gills. Feel

like taking the air?"

"Fucking hell, Pound."

Izzy grinned that same crooked grin, though never so broad as tonight. He set the glasses aside and Noel followed him out. They walked on in silence, the cool air a balm after the steaming pub. Still no relief from the burning in his brain.

"Sorry if I set you off," Izzy said. "But you did insist."

"You ain't told anyone?"

"Not a soul but you."

Even now, under the wavering gaslight, Izzy had never looked more hale. Never by his sheer physical presence make Noel so aware of his own meagre prospects.

One sacrifice, one sin. Repeated, but only the one.

Izzy had hid it for a year.

He ought to walk away. Bid his old friend the best of luck and forget everything he'd learned. There were other ways. Other chances. Surely by hard work and ambition and luck…he would end up right where he was. No amount of carrots or cabbage was going to buy him a tailor-made like Izzy was sporting. Not when every penny Noel earned went to just staying alive.

"Does it hurt?" he asked.

Izzy stared for a tick, then laughed. "Do I have to answer that?"

"No, only…what if I wanted to meet her? Your…whatever. Proprietress."

"Why would you want to do that?" Izzy said, all humour snuffed.

"Well, they say, don't they, variety is the spice of life and all."

"Were you not paying attention just now?"

"What's the difference between you and me?"

"They'll hate you, the custom. For nothing but your colour."

"They hate you too, you slum-dwelling Cockney parasite. Yet they're paying through the nose to get their hands on you."

"What's your point?"

"If they're creaming in their smalls over the fact that you're an East End nobody, a black East End nobody will make them bust on sight." Noel started to laugh, for the whole scheme was ludicrous. Manic. Impossible. Yet there was Pound, hale and hearty, eyes bright. The bugger was happy with his life. "So let's go."

"Go where?"

"To meet that Ursula of yours."

"Not a chance. I told you, it's my night off."

"Tomorrow, then." Before Noel lost his nerve. "I don't expect nothing, just...what have I got to lose?"

For a heartbeat Izzy's face was pinched by unspeakable regret, a taste he wished he need not swallow. Then his old smirk imposed itself, and it was just Izzy Pound in a very fine suit standing under the halo of the gaslight.

"Cobber, you wouldn't believe what a man can lose."

They separated soon after. Noel stumbled home in the same dream state as before, the sounds around him muffled as if his ears were stuffed with wool. At home he stood at his front door for a time, unable to enter. Nothing had changed, not yet. He was still the same man as this morning. It was only after tomorrow that he would be different. Because he was going to follow Izzy's lead and buy his freedom with his...

If only he could think clearly, without interference from his restless body. If only it was just his mind and not also his flesh involved in the decision. If only he was disgusted and not merely disturbed. What was it he wanted? To be so used? To be the user? Or was it Izzy himself who had stirred him?

Izzy, whom Noel had always forgiven, no matter what he'd done. Who had lured him into so much in the past that he could appear out of thin air and convince Noel to change his life in the space of an evening, without even asking.

Except Noel hadn't changed a thing. He'd made no commitments, to Izzy or his affairs. He wanted only to be introduced to the proprietress, nothing more. He was a young man full of untapped passion, easy prey for temptation, and knowing this was what would keep him on the level.

CITY BOY

It was meant to be Izzy's day off, yet here he was on Spencer Street at ten in the bleeding morning no less, sitting in Ursula's office to discuss the terms under which he might pimp his oldest friend.

That's not what this was. This was nothing, a chat, an exchange of information germane to their mutual interests. This was absolutely not him sitting in his procurer's office talking about his friend like he was no more than a set of employable body parts.

"I just want to say again, for the record, I did not attempt in any way to recruit him. He insisted."

"Why did you even tell him?" Ursula asked, accepting a tea from Annie.

"I don't know," Izzy groaned, covering his face with both hands. "What was I thinking? His mother'll murder me."

"Mr Peters is able to make his own choices."

Annie had left him a cup on the edge of Ursula's desk,

on the saucer one of those ginger biscuits he liked, but he had no stomach for anything. In a few hours, his friend would be at the door, waiting to be let in. Into the House, into this life, and while it was better than robbing or fighting or graft, it was still unsafe, still a crime on all fronts, still the bought bodies that would bear the penalty while the buyers paid their way free.

"I dunno, maybe he'll not like it. Maybe he'll wise up."

"Do you believe your own choices have been unwise?"

"No, just… It's not for everyone, right? It's not everyone who can do this night after night." In a minute he'd be talking himself out of it. Yet being off work had been a kind of torture. It was like a drug, a thing he couldn't get by without. He needed to be here. Unlike Noel, who hadn't been infected. Yet.

"I believe you're jumping to conclusions, Mr Pound. There's no harm in Mr Peters meeting me this evening. If he has interest, I would expect him to undergo a similar probationary period to yours. Spend some time in the salon observing the process, the professionalism with which we carry out our business."

"I suppose it's up to him."

"Precisely."

He took the biscuit, bit off the corner. Noel wouldn't be called on for months. Plenty of time for his friend to weigh the costs and come to his senses.

"Ah well, it's out of my hands. But don't forget, if this all goes to shit, that not a bit of this was my idea."

And yet it was entirely his fault. He ought to have left well enough alone, let Noel be. Of all the people whose lives he could have ruined, Noel deserved it the least. Then again, he'd been the only one Izzy missed with any depth of feeling. The only one he'd thought of concretely in the past year. The only one who knew.

One might forgive Izzy for his loneliness. The girls were more than kind, but it was a trial not to feel his isolation. Things that happened on his jobs didn't happen to them—getting the droops, getting scraped by careless teeth, clients telling him he looked like their sons. Indulging the clients' guilt for sinning doubly and their giddy glee at same, at breaking not only moral codes but the law, knowing it was Izzy who'd pay for the crime while they fled to their hunting lodges and summer homes to wait out the scandal of being corrupted by a reprobate.

He bid Ursula good day and went out, even though he had nowhere to go. For the past year his life had run a tight circuit between the House and home, with stops for meals along the route and the odd detour to tailors and shoemakers and such. Noel wasn't due until seven. Given time to himself, Izzy had no idea how to spend it.

Drawn by the clamour and colour amid Mayfair's staid beige and black, he found himself at Speakers' Corner. Today the wedge of open ground on the east edge of Hyde Park had the look of a carnival, orators in impressive hats sporting feathers and flags, one fellow in a scarlet opera cape which he kept flapping like wings as he decried the papacy from atop a wooden crate. A suffragist and her solemn children were selling ribbon rosettes, another more practically dressed family across from them were selling toffee apples, floating above the crowd the domed hats of the bobbies on the lurk for nimble fingers. Everyone save the bobbies were yelling at the top of their lungs.

On into the park for a wander, a half-dozing kip under a tree, his hat over his face, hands crossed on his belly to cover his watch pocket. A packet of peanuts and leaning on the wrought iron railing, watching swans ply the Serpentine. A country idyll for a city boy, though the sky above was the same gritty brownish-grey as ever. Last night with Noel by the river, he'd been able to see the stars.

URSULA

Noel was on edge from the minute he crossed the bridge. More than usual, for there was ever a threat implicit when he dared to mix outside his own neighbourhood. The closer he got to the posh bits of London the less welcome he felt, his quick pace itself a disguise, to make him seem an errand boy on some business of his master's, even though his best garb barely rated good enough for a household servant.

That wouldn't last. He was going to better himself. He was going to accept the costs, and come out the stronger man. He was definitely not going to end in jail, or murdered by a john. Izzy would make sure of it, would protect him as best he could. Which was not at all.

Two complete contradictions: to do or not to do this thing he was proposing. Saying no meant pretending he didn't know. Saying yes meant admitting he wanted it. There didn't seem to be a maybe. Either he turned right at the next corner and cut his friend forever, or he turned left and put his own body on the line.

He dithered, his back to the wall to stay out of the way of foot traffic, his heart in his throat. It might be any one of them he ended up under, any of these men with frockcoats and top hats and parsnip-pale faces and buckets of money and inherited titles and parliamentary seats, passing before him in an endless parade of privilege. And Izzy took it from them, on the regular.

Noel shook himself awake. Across the road, a bobby was eyeing him ferociously. Noel let his gaze slide away, then shoved off the wall and resumed walking, not in haste but not without it. When he reached the corner, he turned left. His body was forfeit already. A pair of dirty hands for digging and a back for bending, and never a damned thing more. To be fucked was at least to be seen. He hoped.

He was in for it now no matter what as Izzy dodged across the street and fell into step beside. He was wearing yet another tailored suit, this one in sleek ruddy velvet. "You ill, cobber?" he asked. "You've gone green again."

"Bit of hostility in the air towards yours truly."

"Never mind that. The House is safe as, well, houses. Ain't no one getting in that she don't want in."

"You said they've got keys."

"*A* key. To *a* door." As they passed a hat-blockers' shop, Izzy fished a brass key from his breast pocket. He stepped out of the flow of pedestrians, then without even a glance to see who might be watching, opened an unmarked door between the hat shop and the next. Stone steps descended into murky darkness. "Go ahead."

"You're shitting me."

"It's not the Gates of Hell. It's a security measure."

"Whose security?"

"Ours. So no one gets in that she don't want."

"How's a woman going to stop anyone?"

"She don't have to." Grinning, Izzy stepped through the door and started down the stairs. Heart a-gallop, Noel followed, closing the door behind him. At once the light improved, the warm flickering of a trimmed lamp.

They descended to a cellar, empty of goods. In the middle of the room was an old wooden table and a chair, where sat the largest man Noel had ever seen, proportioned like an ox, his close cropped head just missing the age-blackened ceiling beams when he stood. Izzy was still grinning.

"Noel, may I present Clyde. Our security measure. He's mute so don't take it personal if he don't ever greet you." The colossus came around the table and put out a hand the size of a shovel blade, shook Noel's with a gentleness that spoke of immense restraint.

"A pleasure to meet you," Noel stammered. With an appraising glance of his lively grey eyes, Clyde bowed his head in reply, then nodded to Izzy and returned to his post, the chair groaning pitifully as he sat down to resume reading the *Evening Standard*.

The wooden staircase in the opposite corner let them into another stone-walled room though this was more pleasant, with rugs on the floor and a neat settee and chair near the pot-bellied stove. Against one wall stood an old writing table, the sides carved all over with vines and fruit, each leg ending in a claw gripping a gilded orb. Later, Noel wondered how he'd seen the desk at all, because once he saw the woman, it was hard to notice anything else.

She was dressed as Izzy had said, in a high-necked outfit

styled like a gentleman's eveningwear, right down to the ruby stud in her black cravat. Styled like a man's, but cut like a woman's, tight to her curves. Of course she was lovely to look at: a classic beauty, firm of chin and nose, her eyes like shards of summer sky. Those eyes...

She stood up, a graceful movement that made him startle and step back. Snorting a laugh, Izzy grabbed his elbow and dragged him towards her. "Buck up, she ain't gonna bite."

Why don't I believe you? She looked as if she might in fact eat him, pursing her petal-pink lips as her gaze swept over him like an icy wind. He put out his hand, met her firm grip, made himself meet her gaze.

"A p-p-pleasure to make your acquaintance, Miss Ursula."

She glanced at Izzy, the corners of her lips bending into the briefest of smiles. "Ursula will do. And how may I address you?"

"Oh. Peters. Or Mr. Peters. No, call me Noel. I don't know."

Izzy was laughing. "And I thought I had the wobbles the first time. I'm going to leave you to get acquainted, how about?" Still chuckling, he made for one of the other doors. Ursula cleared her throat and he froze, his hand on the doorknob. "I know I'm not on the roster. I'm just going downstairs for a cuppa and a prattle with Annie."

"She'll be glad of the company."

"And don't worry, Noel. I think she's taken a shine to you."

If asked afterwards, Noel could not have repeated a word that was said. Options were offered, choices made, none of them binding, the gist being that he would do as Izzy had done, begin as an odd jobber, get to know the people and the place, get inured to the facts. Ursula showed him round the main floor, through the 'salon' where the trade waited for customers, though his mind was too muddled to take in more than an impression of colour and laughter and glittering light. Along the crimson carpet of the darkly panelled corridor, passing numbered doors, behind some of which one could hear business being transacted with much grunting and squeaking of bedsprings. At the toe of the L-shaped hall she showed him another staircase heading up, but whatever they did up there was more than he was expected to know, as she led him instead to stairs that went down into another cellar room.

The same broad dimensions as the salon above it, this room was by far the friendliest. Izzy was there for a start, his heels up on a dressing table, a cup and saucer balanced on his tum as he chatted with a buxom brunette in not very much clothing at all. Citing business elsewhere, Ursula left Noel to make his own introductions.

Rugs lay across the stone floor, these in somewhat poorer nick than upstairs. The furniture as well, an odd mix of bed- and sitting room goods. Candles flickered merrily from polished silver holders, gleaming off mirrors and bottles of perfume. At the far end, two women were dressing, the freckled white girl laughing aloud at something said by her brown-skinned friend. They both looked his way, then the brown girl gasped.

"Is that you, Noel? Noel Peters?"

No. Not Rose Owen. He hadn't seen her in years, had

assumed she'd married. Or died. Or just gone away, not ended here. Not the girl he'd once believed he'd marry, before he'd known what marriage meant.

Owen. Rose Owen. Mrs. Owen. *Fucking hell...*

She was coming towards him, wrapping a thin shawl over her shoulders to conceal at least somewhat the sumptuous swell of her tits. Younger, he would have done anything to be in this very situation. Now he stood trembling, too beside himself to flee as she patted his arm, asked about his parents, his sisters, his garden, all of which he struggled to report, the outer world seeming less real with every moment he spent inside this one.

Izzy came to his aid partway, explained Noel's position, got him to sit, got him a tea, and soon Rose returned to her toilette. The homey atmosphere resumed, Annie and Izzy's every story making the dangers seem less consequential. The House was a locked box. Only permitted clientele might enter, and the rare guest. Ursula had banned a number of them for overstepping her rules.

"Won't they just go someplace else?" Noel asked.

"They're welcome to, but they usually can't get what they're after. We provide some very specific services," Annie said.

"Girls like Rose?"

"If you mean how she looks, then no. If you mean what she does, then yes."

"And what is it she does?"

Neither answered, Izzy inspecting the contents of his cup, his cheeks florid. Annie smirked, looking from one to the other. "Shall I tell him?"

"Suppose he'll find out eventually."

"Tell me what?"

"Rose is a bircher. A topper, as we say around here. They come to her to get run. To get beaten, Mr. Peters. Like dogs. To get shoved around by the sort of person they wouldn't spit on in public."

"Easy there, Annie," Izzy said. "You'll put the wind right up him."

"Best to get it over with, I say. Otherwise it might break your heart later." She waved to Rose who was heading for the stairs, her shoulders gleaming, lips rouged to match the hot coral shade of her gown. She saw Noel looking and blew him a kiss. She might as well have punched him in the chest.

Izzy and Annie were laughing together. Noel needed air, space, distance between himself and Annie's breasts, barely held in by her half-sheer chemise. Between himself and Izzy, who nightly sold his arse simply so he might dress with decency. Between himself and the Noel who was happy in the company of whores.

He shoved his cup and saucer at Izzy, stood up, walked. Found the door, left the room. Found stairs and went up them to the corridor, where every door was a pathway to a new kind of perversion. All of them locked, but one had to lead out, back to sanity. Back to good honest dirt. Hearing voices around the corner, he grabbed at a doorknob. To his great surprise it opened. Despite the unrelieved darkness he ducked in.

To a closet. Marvellous. He ran his hands over the back of the door and found the handle, which popped off in his hand. That had to be an accident. Surely no one was paying to be immured.

What did he know about what men paid for? Rose was a topper. Rose beat men, as if they were dogs. Dear Rose Owen, raised by her auntie as her mum was said to be mixed up in bad business. Rose, whose solos in the choir were all that had held Noel's faith those last few years, before he realized he was going to church out of habit and not belief. Rose, making a rich man kneel, lifting her coral skirts, obliging him to serve her... He moaned, in horror or want, the feelings inseparable.

"What in blazes? I didn't ask for a voyeur. Who's damned well in there?" Noel's heart seized in his chest as a man began hammering on the wall. A chink in the wall panel at eye-height darkened as the fellow leaned in to look.

"I'm certain it's nothing," a Frenchwoman purred. "Now come back and finish what you started or I shall be very cross with you."

"Yes, madame," the man replied in quite a different voice. "I'm sorry, madame."

"Not nearly sorry enough."

The man yipped, a little cry of pain or surprise, echoed by Noel as Izzy yanked opened the door of the closet.

"Let me guess," Izzy said with a grin. "You thought this was the way out."

Ducking Noel's shamefaced apology, Izzy let him out via a second set of stairs from the staff room which led up to an alley. "Head right, and be sly about stepping out." Izzy said, lingering in the doorway.

"You're not coming with?"

"I got some things here to sort out."

"Izzy, man... I dunno if I can do it."

"She ain't asked anything of you."

"Yet."

"Hey, don't fuss. If you can't, you can't. I know you'll keep it quiet regardless."

"I can't believe Rose Owen is..." To say it was to remake his whole past and every future he'd imagined.

Izzy nodded. "I know, mate. That were a right floorer, when I put it together. You used to fancy her, didn't you? Once upon a time." Grinning his crooked grin, he stepped inside and closed the door, leaving Noel in the dark.

THE NEW ONE

HE COULDN'T REMEMBER a worse day. Not a thing went to plan. The night-soil came late, the market pick-up came early, and the rain came continuously. His sister Gladys felt poorly and so they were short a hand. By midday Noel had tripped over every hummock of earth, every fallen stalk, every mole hole between the river and the road, and had spilled the barrow four times, once while it was full of rotted manure.

He didn't complain. He hated every minute, and he never said boo about it. What was there to say? The work had to be done and done by him as there was no one else to do it. Taking Ursula's offer meant leaving his parents and sisters to manage the allotment by themselves. Money wouldn't make the work go away. Wouldn't lower his father's expectations neither, and so Noel would be working from sun-up till past midnight.

Impossible. He'd be dead in a fortnight. Under no circumstances would he be able to tell them where the money

was coming from. Perhaps the Pounds didn't ask questions of their youngest son, having had so many before
him. Noel was the youngest Peters, but the only boy. On
his back rested his family's whole future.

The rain let up as their work was ending. Soaked to the
bone, too tired to blink, Noel sat on his rickety bench and
watched the river and its parade of punts and barges and
low-skimming seagulls. At his father's lumpen tread on the
stone-way Noel shifted to give him space on the bench.

"Nah, if I sit I ain't gonna be getting up again for a
while," he said, leaning his elbows on the handle of his
spade.

"Fair enough."

"You not coming home?"

"Later."

"How much later? Like that other night when you shuf-
fle in at the wee hours thinking I no gonna hear you?"

"Sorry, pops."

"Eh, I can't be too down on you," he said with a shrug.
"It's damn hard, getting by. But you just watch who you
make for friends. Be sure they're friends."

"You no gotta worry, pops."

Cocking an eyebrow, he sucked his teeth at his youngest
child. "Say what you want, boy, I'll worry if it suits me."
He straightened and started up the hill.

"Say goodnight to mum for me."

His father stopped and turned to him. "I ain't gonna
say a thing to that woman. You tell her your damn self.
Like I need her saying to me all night, *why you no stop him,
Lucius? If he die, it all be on your head.*" His spot-on mimic
of his wife's declaiming made both of them laugh. "Just do

the honourable thing and take your licks when she beats the sense back into you."

Once his father had gone, Noel got the bundle of his best clothes from the shed. Ursula had bathtubs. He wasn't going to Ursula's. He was going home, except that he wasn't, was instead crossing the bridge, his best gear in his arms, his every step taking him closer to...saying no. He was going to the House to refuse her offer. Then he would go home, and that would end it. He could die knowing he never gave up that part of himself. Because scrabbling in the dirt from sun-up to sundown to put food on other men's tables was, oh yes, far superior to lying in a bed.

Being buggered. That was why the offer was impossible to take. Because the act was impossible. Because every time he brought to mind what it was he would have to do, he felt wrong all over. Izzy was right, the custom would hate him on principle. Use him to work out their bigoted frustrations, make him the stand-in for the other bodies like his they were no longer permitted to abuse. His own grandfather had been a slave. Cared for, treated with near human dignity, but only by that one man, who had owned his grandfather like one owned a horse or a wheelbarrow. Lied to him with every breath. Left him to be shipped him overseas like a piece of furniture to a family in Kent, who were by all accounts none too happy with the abolition of their ownership shortly after. Hence Noel's grimy hands and filthy clothes and miserable prospects. It was still better to die in his honest dirt than to bend for Tory fucks.

And the first thing an honest man did was sever his ties to the criminal world, formally and completely. Izzy was a criminal. Repeatedly, deliberately, and without apparent remorse. If Noel didn't cut him, and the sooner the better, he would end up the same.

He was fairly running by the time he hit Spencer Street. The shops were shuttered, the lamps were being lit, and a white man in dark clothing was opening an old door with a little brass key. Noel turned his face street-side as he passed, wanting to know nothing of who the man might be.

At the bend of the road, Noel stepped close to the wall and crouched as if to tie his shoe. The man had gone inside, and with a last sweep of the surroundings, Noel backtracked then passed behind the blistered ad hoarding that obscured the alley.

This was the worst he would have to endure, waiting for someone to arrive and let him in. At least he couldn't be seen, and he spent his time trying to scrub the dirt out of his hair. Shortly a woman entered the alley: statuesque, honey skinned, dark of hair and eye. She looked him over as she approached. "You're the new one, are you? Noel?"

"I am."

"Marisol," she said, extending a gloved hand for him to bow over. Then she produced her own key and opened the heavy door. "Come along. Let's get you into a bath, hmm?"

"It was you. Yesterday. You were in that room beside."

"Next time you want a wank, use a suite, silly. Those peep rooms are in high demand."

She indicated the stairs to the dressing room; he was to go first. As much as he wished to be done with this, it wouldn't do to greet the pristine Ursula in his filthy state. Down he went, where he stood by the door while Marisol arranged his bath. In the corner of the room, behind nothing but a chinoiserie screen. While on the other side women loafed about in their underclothes.

A test, that he would not let this get under his skin. Standing, he could see clear over the screen, but Marisol had provided a little stool where he sat to peel off his muddy garb. Then a few dips of water to rinse the worst of the dirt off his hands and arms and the back of his neck. Hand over his shrunken tackle, he stepped into the tub, exceedingly conscious of the women speaking softly on the other side of the screen. As he settled, Marisol returned.

"Shall I leave you to it?" she said, arching one elegant eyebrow.

He sank lower in the water. "If you wouldn't mind."

She snorted, muttered something in French as the door from the salon opened and another woman came laughing into the room.

"Loves, you wouldn't believe it," she called to the gang by the mirror.

"Do tell! Was it Auld Whiskey?"

"Oh, he's was in such a fright. I thought he'd call uncle for certain. Blubbing about some poor sot he'd sacked from the ministry."

"I bleeding hate it when they do that. Like we're their absolution. Get a priest, you wankers."

"Some of them bleeding *are* priests."

"Have you ever had that Monseigneur?"

"Oh, the way it bends?"

As the gang of them broke up in cackling laughter, Noel realized he was holding his breath. They'd forgotten him, or didn't care.

"And the way his balls are—"

"If you wouldn't mind," he called. They were more foul-mouthed than his sisters. The women whispered together, then a curly blond head popped over the top of the screen.

"It's the new one. Girls, look!" She beckoned and two more heads appeared, a sleeker, pinker blond and a girl who seemed carved from ebony.

"Oh, he's a charmer for sure," said the sleek one.

"I 'eard your name is Noel," the other girl said in an even thicker French accent than Marisol's.

"Cor, I think he's blushing."

He was in fact attempting to sink as low as he could in the tub, the washcloth across his middle, his cock making itself most unworthy of their attention. "Can I finish without an audience perhaps?"

"I don't know. Can you?" the sleek one said with a cheeky leer.

"Sophie, let him be," the ebony girl said. "You've only to look at him to know he's *un vrai homme*."

Giggling, they went back to their chatter. He got out quick and rubbed dry, but the bundle of his clean clothes was not on the floor where he'd left it, nor were the dirty ones he'd been wearing. Binding the strip of towel carefully around his hips, he cleared his throat. As one the women turned to stare at him.

"Ah. Uh. I had some things...clothes...which aren't here now...and I'm not really sure..."

"Marisol said you were to wear that," the curly blond said, pointing behind him to a suit of clothes on a stand.

"Can I have my own clothes back?"

"Who did you give them to?"

"No one, I—never mind. I'll just wear that for now."

Everything was there, down to a sleek set of underclothes that caressed him rather more sweetly than was appropriate. The trousers were a little short, the tailcoat a little loose, but as an ensemble it outclassed anything he'd ever worn. So much that his hands were shaking as he adjusted the high starched collar in the mirror by the stairway. For this, Izzy sold himself. Noel would not, wouldn't bend to those bastards. Not even once.

A Matter of Instinct

It was just gone half nine, and the house was alive. Stepping into the salon was like being dropped into the midst of a fantastical circus. Women everywhere, beautiful women in ball gowns and high-swept hair, jewels around every bared neck, smiles on every sweet face. The men paled in significance, standing by the walls in po-faced pairs with their jackets tugged over their pricks. Others, bolder, had sat down with women beside or atop them.

The bar was at the back, recently built according to Izzy in the main to keep a respectable distance between the clients and the non-trading staff. Noel slipped round the edge of the room to reach its sanctuary.

The barkeeper Sal was short and boyish, a thin cheroot clamped in his teeth as he shook the steel cocktail maker with dizzying speed. He uncapped it and poured the foamy concoction into a pair of coupes, making rather a show of it. The man at the bar applauded gleefully, then fished a coin out and flipped it high. Sal snatched it from mid-air.

"Much obliged, sir."

"Come, Erwin, you can tell me about your new horse," purred Marisol to her client. She picked up both glasses and he followed her from the bar. The barkeep looked Noel over quick, then passed him a tray.

"Collect the empty glasses. But be sure they're empty. They pay by the ounce." Perhaps Sal was American, with that flat husky accent. It was easy to obey. Holding a tray made Noel feel less conspicuous, and he made several circuits of the room without incident. Izzy came in but promptly departed in the company of a man dressed just like him and twice his age.

This happened three more times in the next couple hours, with no chance for them to speak, Noel kept in constant motion by the barkeeper's commands. Each time, he watched his old friend for any sign of what he'd just endured, but either Izzy was a master of deceit or he was unremittingly bent, for he smiled, laughed, bleeding well danced, carrying on as if this were the greatest of thrills, the night of all nights.

As midnight approached the tumult wore down. Sal locked up the bottles and went to give the count to Ursula, whom Noel had expected to see at least once. Soon, when he went to get paid. Hopefully his clothes had resurfaced, or he was going to owe...shit.

What a fool he was, about to get extorted for his own clothes. That was their game, to stick him in this situation until he was dying to get out, then make it impossible without some kind of exchange.

"Keeping steady, Noel?" Rose, leaning on the bar, smiling at him like she didn't know. "You don't look so steady."

"Where the hell are my clothes?"

"Likely in Izzy's room. Did she not say?"

"I haven't seen her once."

"I wondered if she'd end up stuck in the office all night. Bit of a roister this evening. They must have passed some bill down the House of Commons to give themselves another pay raise."

"Rose...why are you here?"

"You mean in the trade?"

"Yeah."

She wasn't quite looking at him, spinning one of the rattan coasters around on the walnut bar top. "It was this or the laundry. You know my auntie. You ever see her stand up straight?"

"Did you know your mother, growing up?"

She shook her head, sighed, stood up. "There are no perfect choices, boy. Sometimes it's a matter of which kind of damned you're content to be."

"Amen to that."

"So which you going to choose?"

"You mean between peasantry or purgatory? I dunno. It's hard to trust the upper crust. I just know one of them twits is going to call me a filthy savage and I'll tear him to shreds."

"Perhaps. It's never happened to me."

"They don't make a big deal of it?"

"Me being Jamaican? Here and there. But I don't play into it much. And boy, I and I could be spitting some mad patois, but they wouldn't understand a word of it."

"Izzy said some like him on account of him being poor."

"There are some who will make a fetish of just about anything. It seems nothing is more exciting for a man at the top of society than to be fucked up the arse by a man from the very bottom."

"Wait…Izzy's not taking it?"

"Not that I know."

"He's in charge?"

"Pretty much always, as far as I know."

"And so what about me?"

"What about you? It's your body. How would you like it to be treated?"

"I frankly didn't think I'd have a choice."

"You might not, other places. The House is a cut above. And the custom know exactly what to expect." Rose glanced towards the entry, where a lantern-jawed fellow in a bright blue suit had just arrived. "You'll have to excuse me. He's one of my regulars. And he's bloody well late."

"You going to whip him?"

"Whip if he's lucky. I'm taking him Upstairs." With the promise of that word ringing in the air, Rose patted Noel's arm then walked towards the man with her hands out in joyful greeting. The gent paled, then flushed, then accepted her embrace, stiffening as she whispered in his ear. With a fervid nod, he let her lead him by the hand out of the salon.

Noel couldn't quite breathe. On top. Izzy was the one on top. Izzy ran them. Fucked those toffs' lilywhite arses with impunity. Maybe even beat them. Then took their money.

He set down the glass he'd been drying, before he broke it. "I need…I just…can I…"

There was no one to ask. He left the salon, suddenly sweating, craving air. The corridor was empty and he hurried towards the exit, hearing nothing, knowing anyway. He rounded the corner as someone was leaving a room: Izzy, who smiled upon seeing him, not at all expecting Noel to walk right up and kiss him.

Hard. Square on the lips. Unequivocally, grabbing at his jacket when he made to pull back. Until he softened, swooned into it, opened his mouth. Let Noel possess him, push him against the wall, kiss him and kiss him until neither could breathe, till they clung to each other like drowning men.

"Fucking hell, Peters," Izzy panted when Noel finally stopped for air.

"I had it wrong. I thought that it was you that laid down. I was thinking, for no man would I lay down. Even less for men like that. But would I fuck them?" He grabbed Izzy's chin, tipped back his head to nip at the tender skin of his throat.

His friend moaned, thrust, grabbed for his wrists. "So why are you aiming to fuck me for?"

"I want you to show me. Teach me how."

"It's largely a matter of instinct, to be fair."

"Then let's call this instinct." For it sure as hell wasn't good sense. If pressed, he couldn't have made it make any sense. All he knew was that this was the body he wanted first.

Another door opened and Noel stepped back, unsure of the rules, but the couple were around the corner and stayed out of sight. When he turned, Izzy had gone into the room he'd just left, and Noel followed.

Izzy was sitting on the edge of the bed, his head in his hands, a picture of rather more dejection that Noel was hoping for. "What's wrong?"

He looked up, his jaw set. "Fucking hell, Peters. I've only known you half my bleeding life."

MR. PETERS

HE HADN'T SEEN IT coming, not at all. Then again, Izzy hadn't expected any of what had happened to him this last year. Maybe this was just more of the same, one more peculiar choice he'd never expected to make. A choice been taken away, as Noel's avid smile faded.

"I've mucked everything up, haven't I?" he said, feeling behind him for the doorknob. "I'm sorry, Iz. I'll go."

"Wait!" Izzy was standing—he'd stood and missed doing it. "I didn't say to leave."

"But—"

"But nothing. Stop and talk to me, you twit."

Both an ask and a dare, for young Noel Peters had been a master of the disappearing act, of being there one minute and gone the next, right when you were about to put the hard word on him. He turned from the door, chin jutting, arms crossed, every bit his father's son.

"Go on, then," he grunted. "Talk."

"Very well. What in hell are you thinking?"

He blinked, caught off guard. "What do you mean?"

"You and me have been getting on nicely, everything running tickety-boo, and now you've gone and mucked it all up. What am I supposed to think?"

"You can think whatever you like."

"I'd like to think you're my friend."

"I am your friend."

"Yeah, well, not all friends...you know, plant kisses like that on one another."

"I'm sorry. Was I not any good at it?" He prodded his lips.

"That's not the point. And anyway, I ain't got much to compare to, as far as kisses go."

"Not with all them...clients?"

Somehow it had always been unthinkable, to put his mouth on those grovelling grubs. Somehow it had never come up, as if they knew their place. "Cobber, there's a line," Izzy said, wishing his voice wasn't shaking, wishing for so many things. "There's what they pay for and then there's everything else. And I don't ever cross that line."

"See, that's what I need to know," Noel replied, breaking from his reserved pose by the door, stopping short of grabbing Izzy only by visible effort. "You need to show me."

"Show you what?"

"How to run 'em," he said, a strange light kindling in his velvet eyes. "How you do it. I want you to do to me what you do to them."

A kaleidoscopic vision arose in Izzy's imagination of Noel surrendered, subject to the savagery he unleashed upon the custom. With it came a dizzying fear unlike any he'd known. Baseless, nameless, it struck like a punch and left him reeling. "I can't. Not a chance."

"Please?" he said far too tenderly as he took Izzy's hands. "I wouldn't mind if it was you doing it."

"You don't understand what you're asking. It's not pretty. It's not loving, what happens to them."

"I don't care."

"You ought to care. You ought to be damn well terrified." He stepped back but there was nowhere to go with the bed against the back of his legs and Noel still holding his hands and gazing at him with that new light in his eyes, speaking softly, words for Izzy's ears alone.

"Then let's leave all that be. What if all I wanted was you?" He stepped even nearer so that Izzy had to look up. Look up and be lost in that velvet gaze, in the hot scent of Noel's skin. "What if the rest of it made no difference at all, and the reason I kissed you is because I wanted to?"

"Is that why you did it?"

"It's why I'm going to do it now."

Slowly though, his rough hand skimming Izzy's jawline, tipping up his chin. Holding him thus for one perfect moment of pure longing before bringing their lips together in the sweetest of kisses. Sweet and raw and wet and strong, so strong, Noel's body forged to iron hardness by his life of labour and his coarse hands holding him close and it was only the second kiss of Izzy's love-life and it topped every sensation he'd known.

One needed to breathe now and then, he discovered. Still in Noel's arms, he rested his head against Noel's shoulder, savouring the feel of his hands roving over his body, tracing the shapes of him and tugging at his clothes.

"Please, Iz," Noel whispered, nuzzling Izzy's curls. "Don't leave me wanting."

He shook his head, burrowing into the warm curve of Noel's neck. "I can't do it. I can't be for you what I am for them."

"Just be you, then. That's all I want. I want you."

They kissed again—never enough kisses, now that he'd tasted them. Never enough Noel, who was a quick study if he was new to the art. Another vision arose, the flip side of the coin: himself under Noel, subjugated, spread, begging. Arose and stuck, so palpable, so near to coming true that Izzy's knees buckled.

Noel caught him in a crushing embrace. "Iz, what's wrong?"

"Nothing you won't be able to fix."

"Tell me how."

How to say it, how to ask for what had not existed as even a thought until seconds ago? How could he ask for cruelty, from someone who gave only kindness? How could he want it at all? That last was a question for much, much later. What mattered right now was the asking.

"You're something else, Noel Peters," he said, his throat hitching on the dear man's name. "A cut above all others. I can't imagine being cruel to you."

"So what do you want?"

Izzy reached behind himself and found Noel's hands. Arching against him, he scraped his fingernails lightly over Noel's bare wrists. "You to be cruel to me."

"Why would you want that?" Not a *no*, but a *why*. One hurdle cleared.

"God alone knows," he said truthfully. "All I know is

I've never known a man who stirs me like you do." He swivelled his hips, his stand riding against Noel's, so close, so soon to be his. "Come, Mr. Peters, you must have some idea of what you might do with me."

"Is that how you talk to them?" Noel asked hoarsely as he wrapped his hard hands round Izzy's wrists.

"No. I call them *scum*." He swivelled again, arching under Noel, asking with his whole body. "Tell me what you want, Mr. Peters."

"I don't know," he rasped. "I don't know what I want."

"I suppose not. You ain't been trained yet, have you?"

He grunted a little laugh, the tension easing from his face. "Are you gonna be my instructor?"

"That'd make you my apprentice, wouldn't it?"

"So instruct me. Tell me how you run them."

"You don't want what I do to them. Not for your first."

"Do you whip them?"

"Cobber, I bloody well terrorize them."

What Comes Natural

IT WAS THERE IN his pale eyes: the capacity for harm. Izzy Pound was no longer a skint, scrawny, hard-done nobody, but a man with untold power, who made privilege kneel, who made them suffer. Noel could have that power for himself...

"So?" he said in the gruff tone that seemed to stir Izzy so. "Instruct me."

"Are you going to be a good apprentice and do what your master says?"

"Yes, sir."

Izzy shivered, sucked in a breath. "You don't ever say that to no one but me, right?"

"Gotcha."

"This is for us."

"Always."

For one solitary moment Izzy looked like he might start to cry, a strange contortion of his face, desire so strong it hurt. And then gone in a blink, and nothing left but that power, that crooked grin. "In that case let go of me."

"Eh?"

"So you can get undressed, you berk."

He wriggled from Noel's grasp and went to the dresser. Noel thought to follow him, but his legs had gone soft and he sat on the bed, plucking vainly at his shirt studs with numb fingers. With one kiss he'd started something beyond his control. Had let his curiosity become a compulsion, let the seed of wanting planted in him years ago by this ragged scoundrel grow and bloom and overcome his better sense, run riot in his orderly understanding of the world. He was running out of time to do anything about it as Izzy returned to the bedside, wearing nothing but his shirt and grinning wildly.

"What's that?" he asked as Izzy tossed a little jar onto the bed.

"Our saving grace." With that he whipped his shirt off over his head and sat himself on Noel's lap, straddling his thighs. They kissed again, and it was just as good as all the other kisses. Just as good and just as dangerous.

"Iz…" he started, but Izzy merely hummed in reply, not lifting his mouth from Noel's neck. "Is this wrong?"

At this he sat back to look him in the eye. "By whose measure?"

"Yours."

He pouted, rocking his hips so that his bare cock slid against Noel's belly. "Seems we've gone a bit far down the road to turn back now, ain't we?"

"What'd you mean?"

"At this point, not doing it amounts to about the same as doing it, don't it? That is to say, you ain't gonna wake up tomorrow forgetting that you and me *nearly* fucked, are you?"

"No."

"Then we might as well go ahead and fuck," he said, wriggling against Noel's front again.

"But is that what *you* want?"

Biting back a laugh, Izzy glanced down. "You honestly think I'm faking this?"

"I dunno, I never thought I'd have the chance."

"A chance for what?"

"A chance to have you. You've been on my mind for years, Iz."

He might have slapped him, so great his surprise as he stared at him wide-eyed. "Don't say such things. I never was."

"Honour bright."

"But years?"

"Years."

What followed was one of the most sensually shocking experiences of Noel's life as Izzy undressed him. So very slowly, stopping to kiss Noel's skin as it was revealed inch by inch, teasingly avoiding his cock, swelled to iron hardness and dripping with want. Yet he stayed his hand, let Izzy lead, despite the thrumming, ever-growing urge in his loins to leap upon that lithe, pink body and claim his satisfaction.

Nothing but time now stood between him and that moment, as Izzy crouched on the bed on all fours, his tender body spread to him, his rosy arse...

This, but around Noel's cock...

Kneeling behind him, Noel screwed his twinned fingers

deeper into the hot, clinging depths of Izzy's willing body. "Come on, dolly," he purred, the shake of his hand making Izzy twitch in reply. "Tell me how you want this." Izzy might call the clients scum, but Izzy wasn't a client. Was Noel's plaything, his doll, a thought as natural as breathing now that he'd thought it.

"Fucking hell, Peters—" Izzy moaned, his arms trembling.

"That's Mr. Peters to you, dolly."

"Then please hurry, Mr. Peters" he gasped, his hips jerking, his arse sucking at Noel's fingers. "Before I pop."

"This is a lesson, ain't it? You'll have to give better instruction than that. I said tell me how you want me to fuck you."

"I dunno, just get up behind and do what comes natural."

"Yes, sir."

Izzy groaned, from the humour or from the sudden withdrawal of Noel's fingers. Groaned again as Noel brought the head of his cock against Izzy's softened hole. He began to rock, pushing against some interior constraint, as Izzy responded, pushing back...

Taking him...

Just the head, but by the Almighty...

And then Izzy rocked back again and took Noel in further, and Noel gave it...

Each penetration needed a pause, to come to terms with the intensity of feeling, of need, of disbelief. But here was the proof, their friendship a place in which such miraculous things could happen.

"Sweet mercy..." Izzy sighed.

"Am I hurting you?"

Izzy shook his head, shook all over. "It's been a while. You forget what it's like."

"Is it good?"

"So good..."

"Can I fuck you?" Izzy nodded, another all-over motion. Tensed, gripping the coverlet as Noel pulled back, thrust.

How was there more of him to have? Yet every thrust seemed to spread Izzy more, suck Noel deeper, bring their bodies more completely into union. Moving together, apart, together, and Izzy was making the strangest of sounds, a moaning beyond all emotion, his breath a song he couldn't help singing.

Noel was doing that to him, making him shake, making him sing. He gripped Izzy's hips harder, surrendering to the moment, the both of them damned and so saved. For no Creator could be so cruel as to make bodies to feel this way and then damn them for feeling, for believing this was a sort of paradise...

The climax slammed into him full force, exceeding anything he'd known about how a man could feel. That wasn't spunk gushing out of him and into Izzy, it was all of him, blood and brain and his very soul. He was stupid with it, drunk on fuck, full of idiot thoughts, the shock of the new. A giddying, marvellous shock that had changed his life forever.

And now it hurt a bit, and he pulled out, let Izzy flop groaning onto the bed, where he at once rolled onto his back and began to stroke himself, spurting before Noel came to his senses enough to offer to help.

He lay down beside Izzy, whose eyes were closed, his hand still gripping his cock, spunk drizzled over his bare stomach, the clutch of his pubic hair. After a little he blinked, turned to Noel.

"That weren't bad for a beginner." As Noel drew breath to protest, Izzy chuckled. "I'm joking. That was superb. You might have wrecked me for other cocks."

They kissed once more but softly, Noel ignoring the flick of Izzy's tongue. Insatiable by need or nature? Because he was used to it or because he wanted it? Either way, Noel had no more to give. Izzy neither, wincing as he unadhered his hand from his sticky cock. So much for romance.

"What's so funny?" Izzy asked, struggling upright as Noel chuckled to himself.

"Us. We're a right pair, aren't we?" Izzy laughed along but said nothing more as they rose from bed, cleaned themselves at the washbasin, sorted through their nearly identical clothing. A right pair indeed.

When Izzy checked his watch it was going on one in the morning. Noel was due in the garden at six. So be it; he'd known the risks in coming here tonight. But once he was earning three pounds a night, he could afford to hire in workers. Everything would change. By hook or crook, he'd turn around all their fortunes.

"Will you promise me something?" Izzy said as he stood up from tying his shoes.

"Seems I been doing that a lot lately."

"Fair cop, but look, if this all goes to shit. If the clients are beastly and you can't manage, promise you won't hate me." He was truly afraid, his face pale, eyes too bright.

"Don't look for worry, all right? I'll be fine. I been taking it hard my whole life. I'll be more than happy for a chance to dish it out."

That seemed to satisfy, Izzy back to his smirking self as he opened the door. "Tomorrow we'll have our girl Annie measure you up for a suit. Get you kitted out properly, as befits my apprentice."

"We're carrying on with this apprentice business, are we?" Noel asked as he followed him out to the corridor.

"Indeed we are. Ours is a specialized trade, cobber. You got a few things to learn if you're going to keep your new mistress pleased." He pinched Noel's cheek, then started off down the hall, towards Ursula's office. It was time to get paid.

Monday Night

Days passed, then weeks. Weeks of the strangest services Izzy had yet been asked to provide. Every encounter was a staged performance: the headmaster, the riding master, the raja, which he categorically refused to enact with his face made up brown. If their lordships could suspend their disbelief enough to think him an Indian prince, they could make do with his ordinary skin.

Noel's company sustained him. Not merely his affection in bed but his kind face in the salon, his friendly ear for Izzy's complaints. Of course the affection had much to do with it, for they had discovered a surprising compliment in each other, their desires harmonized, Noel's commanding touch the very thing Izzy had craved without knowing it.

Though it was only Monday night, the House had been crammed with custom, raucous lords carrying on like school boys. Corpulent, overdressed, bewhiskered school boys with whiskey on their breath and deviance on their minds. Izzy got home even later than usual, past three bells by St George's, meaning he could expect at most two hours of solid sleep before his mother began creeping about in the dawn light, doing her utmost not to disrupt the rest of them, failing by dint of the fact that in their narrow flat she was never much more than arm's length away.

As he started up the sagging, damp-smelling stairs of the tenement, Izzy regretted once again that he'd not followed through on his instincts to seek his own lodgings. He had the dosh, the patronage, the bloody need. Yet to leave his family was to give up any semblance of a life outside the trade.

And so he climbed to the top floor, slipped in, waited a few breaths for his eyes to adjust to the gloom, crept past his parents' bed, and sat on the foot of the one he'd shared with his brothers since not much after being born. At least there were only the two of them now. Izzy was the runt, never given the plum spot, always wedged up against the wall so that he frequently woke with plaster dust in his curls. What was he thinking, going on this way? He barely wanted to take off his shoes in his own home. Something would crawl in them, or Pete might nick them, the schemy brute.

Pete seemed to have taken Izzy's own dalliance with—fine, yes, wholesale commitment to—a devious trade as license to let himself fall off the straight and narrow, though in rather a less elegant form, using his speed and whippy strength to work as lookout on a three-card Monty team operating up and down St Katharine docks, fleecing out of towners and locals who ought to have known better. Yet very few coins ever made it from Pete's pocket into the family pot, no matter how swell his garb, how close his shave. Izzy was still getting the girls at the House to do his chin, to spare the expense, pinch every penny.

Shoving his shoes far enough under the bed that they'd be a nuisance for Pete to reach, Izzy flopped back, arms cast over his head, feet dangling. Christ, he could pass out right here, fully dressed, barely even in bed. One more minute and he'd sit up, take off his jacket at least. Once Pete settled down again, as his brother shifted about, grumbling.

Then it started: that jiggle, that rhythm. No. He was dreaming. His heart was racing. Or Pete was scratching his balls in his sleep. Pete wasn't... His brother grunted. The jiggle picked up pace.

"D'you mind?" Izzy hissed.

"Dunno why *you* would," Pete muttered. He sucked in a breath, the bed starting to squeak.

"You're my bleeding brother. Have a shred of decency, will you?"

"Fine talk from the likes of you."

"At least I keep it to myself."

"As if. Lording it over us. All your money. Your fancy clothes. Your—"

Izzy sat up and thumped him on the arm, relishing Pete's grunt of surprise at how hard he could hit now. "So you joined the Life and took up wanking to thoughts of your little brother as a hobby? Marvellous revenge. You sure showed me."

"Shut your bleeding head."

"Go to hell." He shunted down the bed, fished out his shoes.

"Right," Pete hissed. "Run back to your ponce so she

can put you out on the trot again." His enthusiasm waned as Izzy came to stand over the bed.

"Like your minder don't own your arse twice over. Try quitting. I'll send roses to your funeral." Before Pete replied, Izzy punched his shit of an elder brother on the upper thigh, one of Pete's favourite assaults in their boyhood, for the bruise it left where a mother wouldn't look. Then without bothering with his shoelaces, with keeping quiet, Izzy left.

Perhaps for the last time. Briefly he stood in the dark corridor outside their flat, reviewing what of anything he might miss. Childhood dross, ragged clothes. His mother, but not his father. He bent and tied his shoes, then strolled downstairs, suppressing the urge to whistle a tune.

He had never been near Spencer Street at this particular hour, when no one was awake save for the desperate. Whitechapel never truly slept, always someone upstairs or down grumbling or yelling or banging, rifling the rubbish bins or smacking someone else around. In the good bits of town, the streets were desolate. All the better for the rozzers to pluck off those who ought not to be there.

That was no longer Izzy. His apparel alone put him above most reproach. Noel copped more notice, but that was changing, due both to Noel's confidence and to the general sway of England as its black people came ever more into their emancipation. A day would come when one of Izzy's clients would be darker than Noel. Did he really expect to be in the trade that long?

Amused and a little revolted by thoughts of his paunchy, grey-haired self working a geriatric Ursula's salon, it took him a minute to notice his tail. Two of them, which implied a third up ahead, the man who'd ask for directions, a penny, the time so he could get a butcher's at Izzy's watch when he pulled it out to check.

They took him for a swell, which would have been a compliment if it didn't also make him a mark. Izzy fingered the coins in his pocket: a few crowns, enough to put off any beggar, but not these sorts, who were after the lot if they were working in a team. Curse his new high-minded habits that meant his knife was rattling round the drawers in his suite at the House instead of being sensibly concealed about his person.

Six streets from safety, and as the dire train neared the Marble Arch, the third crewman detached himself from its shadows on a course to intercept. Izzy tensed his fists, preparing for what might be the only punch he got to throw.

The third man stepped in his path, his face bland, his cap in hand, though his fingers were hashed by pale scars from a lifetime of fighting. Before he could deliver his distraction, his *might I trouble you, good sir, for the time,* Izzy stepped around him and kept on up the pavement.

"Excuse me—" the man started, as if he'd been insulted by Izzy's refusal to be robbed.

"Sod off," Izzy spat over his shoulder. He picked up his pace, but the buggers kept after him.

"Oi, I'm talking to you!" the one said.

"And I'm answering. I'm no bleeding flat, you schemy shits." Was he going to have to name his connections, remind them how stupid it was to tangle with one of Ursula's own?

Their footsteps sped up. One of them ran at him, but

a life on the brink had honed Izzy's sense of self-preservation to razor keenness. Add to that several months of boxing and a stiff measure of indignation, and under no circumstances was he getting done, not here, not now, not by them, the very same breed as Pete, everything Izzy had pledged himself to never become.

He stopped dead, crouched, pivoted in a single action. Threw all of his weight and his violent momentum behind his fist to crash it hard into his assailant's midsection as he barrelled towards him. The man fell back, clutching his gut and gurgling, and collided with one of his cohort. The third kept on but warily, his own fists raised.

"It's not worth it, Kenneth," the other hissed. "Just leave it."

"Listen to your chum, Kenneth," Izzy grated, poised to fight. "I'm in a devil of a mood."

Kenneth stopped, threw up his hands as he retreated. "All right. Just you mind where you wander at night."

"You mind, you rat!"

His ears ringing, Izzy stalked off, not caring if they saw where he went. Better they did, so they knew whose property they'd nearly damaged. To hell with that. He wasn't property. He was staff. His steps picked up as he came round the corner onto Spencer Street, empty as an unlit stage. He got out his key on the sidewalk where he still had light, then slipped behind the ad hoarding and down the pitch black alley to the clandestine door.

Clyde's night-shift replacement Nellie was there when he got inside. Under the flicker of the dim lamp on the table by the door, Izzy waited for her to approach and sniff him over, fighting a heartfelt urge to scratch the mastiff behind her flappy ears. Never while she was working, Ursula had said, and he respected Nellie's jaws enough to obey. Once she'd done nosing his pockets she snorted like a little bull then padded away to her alcove by the office.

The bawdy was quiet, lacking its usual undercurrent of fucking and frivolity with not a single squeaking spring or grunting man in earshot. Of all the places to feel safe. Too weary to wrestle those particular angels, Izzy stripped to his drawers and singlet, got into bed, and fell asleep on the instant.

THE BEST OF TIMES

IT WAS THE BEST of times, it was…no, it was the best of times, undoubtedly. Noel had it all in balance: his obligations, his occupations, his friendships, his plans for the future. Ursula only needed him twice a week, on Thursdays and Saturdays, lively evenings when the barkeeper Sal found it trying to keep up with the custom, the quality demanding their privileges and prepared to tip well for precedence.

Noel had paid off his tab at the Lion's Head, his in-hand loans. Got his goods out of pawn, though the tweed suit was laughably small, having been in there for almost a year. He sold it to the rag man the next day, as he'd already bought a better one. To his mates around the neighbourhood he said nothing, their expectations on his time already tempered by his keeping farmer's hours. He still played darts with them at the Lion's every Friday afternoon. Still managed church most Sunday mornings, and saints forgive him but it felt good to throw a full shilling on the collection plate and know his neighbours' eyes would pop as it went past to pick up their pennies.

As for the future, it was largely a matter of keeping on as he was and not stuffing it up. With his own debts cleared, he could turn to helping his parents, bring the whole family up with him. Never mind the means. He was only tending bar.

When Noel got in that Thursday, Izzy was there already, seated at one of the dressing tables in the staff lounge in only his trousers and a close-fitting undershirt, curls slicked back hard, chin and one cheek thick with lather, getting a shave from Sophie. The fizzy blonde was a dab hand with a razor, the best barber in the House, and the only woman who scared Noel more than Ursula did, for she was known to use a blade on certain clients. Under rigorous conditions, but still his balls tended to suck themselves up into the safety of his pelvis whenever she was about.

"Howzit, Noelly?" she said. "Your man here's about done." As she wiped the blade, Izzy glanced up. He closed his eyes again as she set it back on his skin.

"What do you mean, my man?" Noel said, his chest strangely tight, his neck hairs prickling in sympathy as she drew the shining blade up Izzy's throat.

"I don't mean a thing," she laughed. "If anything he's a boy. Scared to leave the House, he is."

"You don't have to go round advertising," Izzy muttered as she made him turn his head.

"What you mean, scared?" Noel asked, feeling more peculiar by the moment.

"She don't mean nothing. I'll be up in a shake."

He returned upstairs to Izzy's suite where he'd been keeping his clothes, as he didn't rate his own room until he was earning. Until? More like if he ever got the nerve. Taking money from a bawdy house to do chores and such was miles and miles distant from working *for* a bawdy. Bordello. Pleasure house. Whatever you wanted to call it, for Ursula was an expert at not naming what they did. The johns were *clients* or *custom*, Izzy and the others were *staff*, everything was *requests* and *refusals* and *negotiations*, countless clever ways to avoid saying the words *fuck* or *whore* or *money*.

Yet Noel kept showing up for work. He trusted Ursula because she had never once made him feel obliged to do so. That's not how crims usually worked. Izzy's own brother had been completely collared into the rogue's life, by now had likely witnessed enough down at the docks that he couldn't be trusted not to grass unless kept in fear of the repercussions if he did. On the general scale of criminality, whoring was morally no worse than aiding card sharps in fleecing fools. It was, by Ursula's word, up to Noel what he did next. For tonight, enough to get into his tailcoat and such, prepare for several hours behind the bar pretending to be amused by men of staggering wealth and power and stunning poverty of intellect and integrity. The gratuities were good, though.

Izzy came into his room, his chin fairly shining from Sophie's blade. He locked the door, tossed his towel on the chair to the side. Noel was in nothing but his smalls, his response to Izzy immediate and bluntly obvious. Maybe his friend still wondered why, but to Noel it was a given that every working night began this way, with this whizz-bang eruption of raw desire, as without a question, without even a word, they met in the middle of the room to kiss as if they'd thought to never see the other again, Izzy clinging so hard to him that his braces scraped Noel's bare chest, his mouth utterly open to the thrust of Noel's tongue. Desperate for sensation to drive away the fear.

Noel knew his friend's fear, could taste it the next day when Izzy had pushed himself the night before. Been too cruel. Said something beyond the pale. Done something he disliked, and for nothing more than money.

This Izzy was terrified. Desperate. Should be talking about what was eating him up, instead of using Noel's body to make him forget. Later, when this need had been sorted and Noel could think again.

He grabbed Izzy's hair, pulled his head back, ran his tongue over his freshly shaved throat, still bitter with skin tonic. Used his teeth, for the sound Izzy made, that half-sobbing groan.

"How do you want me?" Izzy panted.

Noel brought his lips to Izzy's ear, making him shiver. "I'm no client. You tell me. Soft or hard?"

"Hard."

"Ugly?"

"Yes."

"Like last time?"

"Fuck, yes."

They kissed again, a near painful clutching, then Izzy dropped his braces, let Noel strip off his trousers. Smalls as well, Izzy at his best when starkers, the new muscles standing out on his sleek frame. Noel put one hand on Izzy's chest and walked him backwards until his legs struck the side of the bed. Izzy sat, then slid down to kneel on the floor, his back against the mattress. Noel moved in, brought his pearling cock to meet Izzy's mouth.

Pinned, Izzy opened, accepted. Took him deeper, whimpering softly around Noel's shaft. As for Noel he had merely to lean in, his hands braced on the bed behind Izzy's head.

He bumped his hips forward, making Izzy moan again. A sound he could feel, a vibration traveling up his cock with every half-pained noise he drew from the other man. Izzy clutching his thighs, Noel thrust again. "I need it. I need to fuck your mouth. Right now."

"Mm-mmh."

"That sounds like a yes..." Too late if it wasn't, the need a burning pyre within him and a sizzling sensitivity without. As if the sucking heat of Izzy's mouth was the centre of all things, this feeling the very reason Noel had been born a man, so that he could do this, feel this, fuck this gorgeous mouth without mercy or remorse.

Beneath him Izzy writhed, his own hips moving in time, helpless tears beading at the corners of his eyes. Too good, too good to be true, too good to last, and with a string of meaningless curses Noel tipped past the edge, his balls seeming to turn inside out with the force of his spending, Izzy's whimper suddenly thicker as he gulped down Noel's cream.

No lingering, and after a few last convulsive humps Noel pushed away, leaving Izzy slumped against the bed, eyes closed, lips flushed and sticky, his unsated cock standing up livid against his belly, this one of their private agreements, that Izzy should wait for permission before touching himself. He stayed this way as Noel went to the washstand and began to wash up.

For all his fierceness in the moment, he never much liked the aftermath, when the only proof he hadn't hurt his friend was his friend's own assurance. Izzy looked martyred, lolling there like St Sebastian all roped and pierced, with the same look of slack jawed delirium, though he blinked to life easily enough when Noel offered his hand to help him to his feet.

"Pity the first chap who gets me to himself tonight," Izzy said with that lopsided grin.

"You in a mood?"

"You put me in one. Better mood than I've been in for a tick." He touched Noel's cheek but didn't kiss him, only turned and went to wash.

"Speaking of moods, what was Sophie on about?" Noel said, sitting on the bed to pull his drawers on.

"Nothing much," Izzy said over his shoulder. "I was on my way back the other night when some jokers took me for a swell, tried to turn me out."

"Who was it?"

"Dunno. People I never seen."

"From out of town?"

"Dunno."

"You all right though?"

Izzy shrugged, taking his time drying his hands, finger by finger. "It weren't the best of nights already. My shit of a brother…" He sighed, shook his head. "I haven't stopped home since."

"Since Monday?" No wonder Izzy's skin looked like wet newsprint, liked he'd had the life bleached out of him.

Noel would lose his mind without a daily dose of seeing the sky. "That ain't healthy."

"Yeah, well, neither is getting jumped by mutchers. Or frigged on by my idiot brother."

"Come again?"

HE HAD INTENDED TO keep quiet about Pete, but Noel was the only one whom Izzy might ever have told, and so while they dressed he told him, about that and the near miss with the gang after. The telling left him out of sorts, the bonhomie of the fuck fading too soon when he'd counted on it carrying him through the night. But he'd have Noel with him all the way, to flirt with and commiserate, now that Noel was getting to know the custom by both face and name.

Which itself was an itch he couldn't help scratching. He'd not brought it up with his friend in near a month, despite how often he got an earful from Ursula about how well Mr. Peters could be doing for himself, if he ever chose. Facing another weekend of professional glee, Izzy could be forgiven for wondering how much longer he'd have to go it alone.

By God, did Noel ever polish up good, the white of his collar and cuffs striking a perfect contrast between his jet black tailcoat and his darkly burnished cheek, his earthy hands. It was almost alarming to witness the custom's hunger for this man whom they'd likely spurn on the street. A man their grandfathers could have legally owned. Reason enough for Noel's reluctance, to not trust any man who didn't respect his personhood. As much as the toffs ever did with persons they were paying.

Sorted, suited, ready for their night's work, they performed their other little ritual, going over each other's suits for lint and loose threads. Izzy was largely in it for the chance to run his hands over Noel in a posh get-up, the tailored trousers cutting close to his excellent backside, which Izzy pinched for luck.

Noel chuckled, caught his hand and pulled him near. Kissed him, his other hand to Izzy's cheek. One last kiss to get them both through, and so they made it last, both of them needing the proof that they each mattered, if only to one other person.

Then it was time. The coverlet was askew, here and there things out of place due to Izzy's having lived in the room continuously for three days. They went about and tidied it back to stark impersonality, stowing his watch, a handful of coins, his pocket knife and such in the lockbox nailed into the bottom of the dresser.

"How long you planning to stop here?" Noel asked as Izzy hid the key behind the loose trim atop the doorframe

"What, live here? Dunno. Till I figure something else out. What about you, though? You ever still think about coming out from behind the bar?" An itch he couldn't keep from scratching.

His face hot, Noel was suddenly quite interested in his fingernails. "Dunno. Yeah. Dunno though."

"Better tell her."

He looked up, wide eyed. "Why? Will she want not want to keep me on?"

Really he ought not to even know his friend's affairs, but

Ursula herself kept bringing it up. "No, it's just she's got a queue. Gets any longer she's gonna lose face."

"You're joking."

He wiggled his eyebrows. Noel's face got even hotter. "Better go see your employer, Mr. Peters."

"Yeah, well, you're coming with, cobber. All of this is your fault, innit?"

"Fucking hell, Peters." Izzy went for his watch, but of course he'd left it so not to have it damaged. "Fine, but we're going right now. I'm on the clock in twenty."

THE LIST

Ursula showed him the list. There they were, fifteen names. No, titles. Those weren't even their names but their bleeding titles. Two dukes, three marquesses, a boatload of baronets, a French count, and a scattering of other excessively powerful men were all angling for a crack at Noel.

Seated beside him on the sofa in the outer office, Izzy was saying nothing, his hand over his mouth, laughter in his eyes. Fucker. He could at least have had the decency to be impressed. The only one Izzy'd had chasing him was Sir Carey *borrowed-my-wife's-prestige* Morwell, whose privilege of entry to the House had recently been revoked for a host of reasons.

"You are, it appears, rather sought after, Mr. Peters," Ursula said. She sipped her tea then set the cup back on the saucer poised on her knee, her typical serene self, pale hair netted high, mannish garb tailored to perfection. Noel had necked his tea in two gulps and his mouth was still dry.

The paper trembled as he returned it to her.

"I wouldn't know where to start." There, proof he had no idea what he was on about, in his having said something so idiotic. Ursula put her tea on the side table then took a slim ledger from the same and returned the paper to it, her every move calm, as if none of this was to do with Noel selling himself.

But he wouldn't be. He'd be on loan. No. He'd be doing a service. Like keeping bar, only more serving. He regretted bringing Izzy into this meeting. There was now too much between them. Saying yes to Ursula was like saying no to Izzy, depriving him of his last friend who wasn't up to his neck in the trade.

Into the stilted silence, the glass-domed clock on the bookcase began to chime. Izzy chuckled, got to his feet, clapped Noel on the shoulder. "I'll see you out there when you're able to tear yourself away from this riveting conversation." He nodded to Ursula and went out, still laughing.

Noel did not feel the least bit better. Not the least bit clearer about what he ought to do. He was not used to feeling like he had control. That was what this was: control over people more powerful than him. People who wanted something only he could give them.

Ursula wouldn't betray him, not now. She was among the most deeply moral people Noel had ever met, treating the clients as disposable and her staff as a sort of family. The House of Lords could not have functioned, as a business or lifestyle, without her steering hand. Her diligent protection. Her paying what must be a staggering outlay in bribes to the police, in the name of keeping them all safe, from arrest and from interference.

He picked up his cup, but it was still empty, and he set it down with a clatter. "I ought to say something, right?"

"Sal will need you soon, yes."

"Right. Fuck. Sorry. It's just…"

"It's a lot to consider. Those are some intimidating individuals," she said, indicating the ledger and its list.

"Any one of them could buy and sell the lot of us."

"And yet they come to us. On their knees, at times. Asking for what they can only get from us."

"Right. I just… I've not done that sort of thing before."

"Your experiences with Mr. Pound notwithstanding?"

"I'd so rather you not bring him into this." Sure, Noel was the one who fucked, often with severity, and Izzy was the one who took it, sometimes with even less grace than this evening, but whatever was between them was streets away from anointing a duke's back with a riding crop, and then… "Sorry, you were saying?"

"Mr. Pound calls you his apprentice, does he not?"

"Bit of a joke, in truth. If I had to call anyone master, it'd be you."

So she did blush. Noel had never seen it, the effect startling, her bone-pale complexion set with two perfect roses. "Thank you. I don't know that it's so, but I'll take it in the spirit it was given."

"So now what?"

"So what if your master asked you to observe our Mr. Pound whilst he provides some typical service? I've a few who like being watched. Some who are on this list. Some who I expect will visit this evening. And so if it happened that you were inspired at the time, you could almost certainly obtain the client's consent to observe. You'd have a much better idea of what I'd expect of you. It is, I suspect, not at all like what you share with Mr. Pound."

"Yeah, he ain't usually—wait, how do even you know what goes on?"

"You gentlemen are sometimes rather loud. It's simple to make out who's who."

"Ah shit."

"Don't be ashamed. We all think it's rather sweet. I think you do him good, Mr. Peters."

"I think so too."

"Then I leave it for you to decide between you how to proceed. Mr. Pound knows my feelings on the subject."

"Right. All right, suppose I'd best be getting to work. Thanks for the tea."

She inclined her head in dismissal. Stepping into the panelled corridor, Noel realized he'd gone through all that only to be back where he'd started. It was still entirely his choice to make. Only now he knew what awaited him. Who it was that wanted him. If Ursula got her way, he was looking at a chance to fuck a thousand years' worth of England's history right up its entitled arse. He hoped England left good tips.

THOUGH HE HADN'T WANTED to be there at first, Izzy wished he'd gotten to hear what Noel and Ursula had discussed. He could guess, as Noel's face was ashy and he spent the first half hour of the night with his back to the room, polishing glassware that already looked mighty clean.

Izzy let him be, having little to say that wouldn't put him even more on edge. Add to that the tenderness of Izzy's throat after Noel's untender ministrations, and he himself was content to sit back and let the show unfold before him, the darkly clothed men and the jewel-like women meeting, greeting, flirting, departing together. Like a stage play: The Wants of Man, the paid sex an allegory for, lessee, Lust and Avarice. Sloth as well, for the clients were exchanging money for the right to not have to put in the effort to seduce the women they were about to bed.

It was quiet for a Thursday, so much that Marisol was leading a game of canasta at the round table near the bar. Izzy had his regulars though, and the expectation of a specific client of particular interest to Noel, as it was one of the lords on that list. Merely a baronet, but anywhere outside of Ursula's domain, the man had wealth and authority enough to get almost any other man condemned, tried, convicted, and jailed if not hanged, with little more than a few whispered words and a barrow-load of sterling.

Izzy was going to beat him till he wept. He'd quiz him on what else he wanted before they got into it. The beating was the main thing, the *casus belli*, to ply a military metaphor as so many of these men loved to do.

The baronet strolled in at half ten, dressed in tails and white tie like he'd come from the opera. He made a circuit of the room as if it were any Mayfair salon, greeting the women merrily, nodding to the men who by and large lowered their eyes or looked in another direction. The twit. Beating was too good for some.

Izzy had been watching the card game, loafing in an armchair near Marisol, teasing her about her draws while she played with unruffled aplomb. The game ran not on money but favours, and Marisol played to win, attested to by the stack of chips beside her. Izzy waited for the man to come to him, then waited for the round to conclude before acknowledging him standing at his elbow. Power, raw and extraordinary, made no less intoxicating by the fact that it was given on purpose.

On the street, he'd be hat in hand, bowing and scraping and saying *milord*, begging for the slightest acknowledgement from this stuffed vest. Here, he looked askance at the baronet waiting on him, the slight man's cheeks pink, teeth chattering, all over him the straining air of desperation. Such delight in this power that Izzy contemplated saying no, the way one might hold a coin in the hand then decide not to spend it. But the only way he got the coin was by saying yes. Better make it count.

"Evening, Morrison. You're looking well."

You could watch how it cut him, being called nothing but his name by one such as Izzy. That was of course the point, to make him catch his breath, bite back the *how dare you speak to your betters thus*. Knowing how dear that would cost him. Izzy was already preparing to tan him something fierce.

"Ah, yes. Thank you, Mr. Pound." That cost him too. Fuck, Izzy was getting hard off this alone. He shifted in his seat to make it more apparent. The baronet glanced at Izzy's lap, stepped back. The nancy...

"Beg pardon, Marisol, you'll have to win without my help from here. Morrison appears to have something caught in his throat."

"Better help him get it out," she said while her long

tanned fingers rifled the cards. Morrison made an odd little squeak, stepped back further as Izzy got up.

"Have a seat." He gestured to the chair. The man swallowed, then sat abruptly. Standing over him, Izzy chucked him under the chin. "I'll come back for you in a tick. Try and behave yourself."

He went to the bar from where Noel had watched the whole act. "D'you know who he is?" Izzy asked, leaning on the rail.

"Should I?"

"He's on that list." He quietly named the man, his title. Noel stiffened, then set down the glass he was holding, his eyes flicking between Izzy and the pink-faced lord in the chair.

"Ursula said to expect one or two of them tonight."

"Well, there's only the one, and he's here now." Noel was breathing hard but he hadn't said no, and Izzy decided to press. "He's an ideal candidate, him. Never crosses a line, not a bad looker. You'd only need to watch."

"What, go with you right now? Who'll mind the bar?"

"The barkeeper. Howzit, Sal?"

"Same as ever," the diminutive barkeeper said with a wink. That was another floorer waiting for Noel, figuring out Sal, who was already enough of a head twist with being American and as slight as a jockey. Grinning, they glanced over at the baronet simmering in his seat. "Can I get you and your, uh, date a little something?"

"Who, Morrison? Nah, he's a teetotaller. He's just here for the suffering. I'll have a quick brandy though. It'll insult him something grand to smell it on me."

"Fucking hell," Noel muttered, more admiring than

afraid.

Izzy picked up the chartreuse glass filled with oily liquor and regarded Noel over the rim. "So, Mr. Peters, you want to come and watch me rain hell on a peer of the realm?"

Noel looked at the baronet. Back at Izzy. "I don't gotta touch him?"

"If he's after what I think, I won't even have to."

"I can just watch?"

"Yeah." Izzy tossed back the drink, barely tasting it, needing only the burn, the heat. "As long as you know, cobber, I ain't like I am with you, with them."

At last Noel smiled, shaky but it was there. "You worried about scaring me?"

"The thought has occurred."

He smiled wider, his face back to gorgeous life. "Just don't change how you are with me, and we're good."

Izzy would have given every penny he had to grab Noel and kiss him, right here in front of everyone. Instead he touched his arm, pledging silently to protect this darling man, every way he could. "Head upstairs. Room number seven."

"What's the gambit?"

"You'll figure it out. We'll be along in about ten. Make sure the fire's lit."

Noel nodded, took a deep breath and blew it out. He squared his shoulders, then with a nod to Sal, headed off. Izzy waited to hear the salon door close behind him before he pushed the glass towards Sal for one more dash of courage.

UPSTAIRS

Noel had been upstairs twice, and never alone. Downstairs, there was always a bit of noise leaking into the panelled corridor, from the salon or the suites; talking, laughing, fucking. Upstairs was very quiet, the rooms very specific, none with an actual bed in Noel's shaky recollection of Ursula's kaleidoscopic tour. The staff made much to the custom about their keys, but the doors upstairs all answered to the same silver one as what let staff into the House.

The doors were weighty walnut jobs, thick with joinery, engraved plates on each to show the numbers. Behind door number seven, the lamps were lit and the hearth burning brightly. Who was it that achieved these magic touches—the laundry, the fire, the cleaning up? He'd ask sometime, when damage wasn't imminent.

None to him. Not physically. Spiritually, though, he had to consider if witnessing Izzy dole out cruelty was a risk too great. He needed Izzy, pathetically, completely. Needed his friendship, his touch. Needed him in truth for someone to pity, as someone who was worse off than himself. Was that what Izzy saw in the clients, the men he harmed?

Noel went about the room, inspecting the bookshelves though he knew none of the titles. On the corner of the heavy desk sat a globe, the mountains done in raised bumps of resin, alongside a ledger the size of a church bible, an inkwell, a clutch of nibs in a glass, a ruler and some other bits of a maths set. Laid across the front of the desk, impossible not to see, a bamboo cane the length of Noel's outstretched arm.

The headmaster's suite. Fucking hell. Not of a school Noel might ever have gone to, but a public school of the Eton variety, where the future leaders of the empire went to learn how to do what they were told.

In the corner was a grand armchair, all green leather and brass studs and a high curving back. From here Noel would have a perfect vantage of the whole scene. For that's what it would be. Not real, not for either of the men, but a fake-out, a sham, a performance. Thoroughly unconvinced, sweating from the fire's heat and all the implications, he hung his jacket on the stand by the door then sat in the armchair. A minute later, the door opened and the other two came in.

The client—a baronet, a man who knew the Queen, who through his wealth and privilege could have shot Noel dead in the street with impunity—hung his hat then went to stand in front of the desk, his hands clasped behind his back. Izzy stopped to take off his jacket, hanging it beside Noel's. He laid his hand on the sleeve for a moment, then he came to the chair and bent close. "You right?"

Noel nodded, wishing like he never had that he could pull Izzy to him, kiss him, claim him. Save him from his own choices. Izzy smiled, touched Noel's face, one butterfly's brush of his fingertips, and Noel's heart fluttered in reply. Too late, as Izzy went to the desk to do what he was about to do.

Unhurried, he pulled out the master's swivelling chair and sat down, then opened the ledger with a deliberate bang. He took the ruler and began going down the lines, searching for a name. "Ah. Here we are. Oh my..." He tutted, shaking his head as the other man's neck got redder and redder. Izzy took up a pen, fitted the nib, opened the inkwell, made a mark in the ledger, muttering disappointments under his breath. The other man began to tremble.

Izzy at last set aside the pen, folded his hands and regarded the baronet across the desk. "Now, Morrison, you may have thought that what with your being an heir, your father's influence and all, that you could get away with your persistent insolence. That was a grave miscalculation, young man."

Izzy's voice had changed, barely a hint of his Cockney clip. Acting. He got up from the desk, circled round the trembling man. "In fact, of late you've been so frightfully disobedient that we've brought the superintendent Mr. Peters in as an observer, to be sure you receive the appropriate measure of discipline."

Izzy's posh voice was doing peculiar things to Noel, stirring his innards, making his heart race though he sat calmly in a chair. He could do the same, as he had before when he dropped much of his parents' West Indian cant. One's speech was a matter of upbringing, of habit, of teaching oneself to carefully say such things as *a pleasure to see you again, Mr. Pound. Might I trouble you to lower your drawers and grasp your ankles so that I might cleave you in half with this unruly prick of mine?*

Not a thing like that happened to the client. The encounter remained as it was, a bizarre replica of a student's worst day. On a large slate on an easel Izzy made the baronet write lines: *I must not suck cocks.* For every time Morrison's cuff smeared the chalk, he received a strike from the ruler on his palm. Then Izzy made him recite *Ode on a Grecian Urn*, counting the stammers and marking them on his other palm. No wonder the upper class were off their collective rocker, inculcated as they were from the cradle to accept and mete out punishment without regard for how it ever fit the crime.

Next, the baronet was made to read a prepared statement on his own wickedness. False crimes, schoolboy crimes, if one's school was sadistically bent: leaving bed after lights out to lure his classmates into indecency, trading sexual favours for tuck shop privileges, propositioning the Games master then failing to do his duty by it.

"I ask, sir, that I be shown no m-m-mercy in deciding my punishment. For it is by your hand…oh God…"

Izzy had the cane in hand and struck him across the calves. "Get on with it, Morrison, other pupils are waiting."

"Yes s-s-s-sir. Your hand that I shall be guided back to the path of righteousness. God, they'd have never made us read something like—ah!"

Izzy had struck him again. "You're not at that poxy school anymore, boy. Good thing too. They've done you a disservice. If I'd had you from the start I'd have never let you become so wicked."

"Yes, sir."

"Take your place."

"Yes, sir." This last a whisper, as the baronet stepped back from the desk to bend forward and set his hands on the edge. Izzy put his hand on the man's neck and bent him further. He glanced one last time at Noel, then went to work.

Thirty strikes? Noel quit counting at a dozen. It was not a swift process. Before long the baronet was in tears. Izzy paused, leaned over him. "My word, Morrison, are you blubbing? You're even more pathetic than I thought." The next vicious strike made him start crying for real. Was this even erotic? Noel felt misled, his arousal at the start a trick to get him to accept this performance as a sexual act.

When he was done, Izzy put the cane back on the desk, an inch from the other man's fingertips, as if daring him to take it up and retaliate. He did not, only pushed himself upright and resumed his original pose, his hands behind his back, the palms cherry red, the whole of him shaking. Izzy sat and flipped open the ledger, made a careful mark then set down the pen.

"You will return to your dormitory. And conduct yourself properly from here on. My patience, Morrison, is not infinite. You'd do well not to try it again."

"Yes, sir."

Izzy made a shooing motion. The baronet bowed, then crossed the room like the floor was not to be trusted. Trembling all over, he took his hat from the stand, unlatched and opened the door and slipped out.

The moment he was gone, Izzy slumped in the creaking chair like the bones had been yanked from his body. His own legs unsteady, Noel hobbled to Izzy's side.

"Are you all right?

It took him a moment but there was that grin. "I reckon that fiver I just made will go a long way to ease my troubled soul."

"Five pounds, and you didn't even…"

Izzy splayed his hands, equally bemused. "Don't ask me. I just work here." He stood up, took another deep breath, flexing his hand. "First time I went that hard at a fellow, I got sick after."

"I have to admit, it's made me much less confident in the fate of the nation."

"That nut-jobs like him are at the tiller? Too right, cobber. Too fucking right. Now go on downstairs. I mean right down. Don't put yourself back out there straight away. Make a tea. I'll catch up with you in a while."

"Not without a kiss."

Izzy coloured, looked away, as if that was the very last thing Noel ought to want. Fine, if he was going to disbelieve, Noel would try twice as hard to convince him. Not with words, for none of the things that wanted saying were worth saying in this moment, when a kiss could say so much. And so he pressed his lips to Izzy's, until his darling softened and flung his stiff arms around him and returned his kiss with all his passion, their bond a thing no man could sunder.

The night never picked up much, and by midnight Sal gave Noel leave. Rather than loaf about the salon trying to ignore every time Izzy left the room, he went down to the vacant staff lounge and dozed away the last hour on the divan in the corner.

It didn't do him much good, laying in the semi-dark listening to the footsteps in the salon overhead, his mind returning ceaselessly to that room one more flight up, the others like it. Like the world reversed, this cluttered, homely belowground room a paradise, the salon a kind of purgatorial realm where one waited to enter the hells Upstairs. His head throbbed, a sour pinching across his forehead. He'd not eaten enough today, had spent too much of it immersed in this life he was still unsure he had the strength to live.

BENT

THE ROOM WAS EMPTY. It ought not to have cut him so hard, that Noel had gone home to his comforts. More bed for Izzy. No prickling conversation, at least not yet. He had until Saturday, two days, an age from now.

Mercy, was he ever tired, the distance from the door to his bed a trek almost beyond him. Yet he bounded to his feet the instant he heard Noel's key, was at the door before it was open. Later he'd think about why he cared so much, after he'd gotten what he needed, which was this kiss.

The best was always when Noel's stiff surprise gave way to his passionate response. As if he was never quite sure Izzy meant it until he felt his tongue teasing his lips to open. And then it was like drowning, if drowning was like a dream, Noel sucking the very breath out of him, crushing his chest, dragging him under.

Then he stopped, leaving Izzy clinging to him, legless as a drunk. "I been waiting for that," Noel purred.

"Wha', all bleeding year?"

"Feels like."

As Noel sat on the bed Izzy started undressing. "Go ahead with your questions," he said, unpinning his tie. "I'll be out like a light soon as my head hits that pillow."

"All right," Noel said in a low voice. "Are you bent?"

Izzy froze. Pivoted on his heel, unable to keep his incredulity from his face. "Are you not?"

Noel shrugged, pursed his lips. "I dunno. There's Rose, right? I used think about her all the time. So what kind of man does that make me?"

"I dunno, a man." Noel tsked through his teeth and Izzy turned to him again. "Slightly bent? Dented? What do you want from me? A badge to wear? A little flag you can wave at Jubilee?"

Noel hissed again. "You're being a cunt."

"Which you like to fuck."

"Damn it, Pound—"

Izzy threw up his hands. "What else is there to say? Go ahead, ask Ursula if you like. She'll give you all this palaver about gametes and fish spawn and the structure of the infant mind, but it just whizzes past me. What I say is, I've got no faith in a God that's made me as I am and then wants to punish me for it."

"You think God did this to you?"

"Who else? Look, if I thought there was any good in it for my soul to play at marriage and such with a woman, I'd do it and save myself a lot of bother. Not to mention a lot of plain old fear about getting my head coved in or my neck strung up. But either there's only a particular sort of woman that holds any charm for me and I ain't met her yet, or that particular woman is a man."

He was talking too loud and turned back to the dresser. If he drove Noel off, what on earth was left for him to hold to? But his friend let it alone, and by the time Izzy was down to his smalls, Noel had already got under the covers. Natural like, as if he belonged there.

Izzy doused the lamp. Guided by memory he felt his way to the bed. As he laid down, Noel slid close and put his arm over Izzy, settling his chin on his shoulder.

"Mind what I said. Sleep first."

Noel's laugh shook the mattress, his breath tickling Izzy's ear. "Be honest. Have you really got no desire at all for women?"

"Well, there's been the odd professional obligation. But that's another thing entire. And cobber, I only got so much desire to spare for the clients, right? I mean, they ain't you."

Noel laughed again, though his arm tensed around Izzy's waist. "I dunno why you're so fixed on me."

"Neither do I, except you're the most like me, not just here but anywhere round. Known you half my life, I have."

Noel propped up on his elbow, all shadows save the pearls of his teeth, his bright eyes. "Come live with me."

Izzy's turn to laugh. "What, and be your love?"

"You can't stay here. You'll go barmy, stewing in here day and night."

"I can't go home."

"I know. Look, I've a cousin who's just enlisted. He's giving up his room over Charing Cross way. A nice one above a dry-goods shop we can maybe get into easy."

Izzy stared up at him, head and heart twisted by the

switch from questioning his motives to wholesale commitment. Noel bit his lip, ducked his head, chuckled again. "Yeah, go ahead, say it, that I'm hoping to get into more than your room."

"Not exactly what I was thinking."

Noel didn't press him, instead moved his hand up Izzy's side, over his chest, to trace along his collarbones, draw out that shiver he liked to cause. "You were a right stunner before. Upstairs."

"Stunner?"

"That voice?" Noel closed his eyes, savouring. "Gorgeous. Powerful. Funny thing is, I wouldn't ever want you to do anything like that to me."

"I wouldn't. I couldn't."

"Besides which, ain't I the one meant to be learning to get powerful men on their knees?" From the bones he moved his hand up to rest on Izzy's throat, so much implied, so much held at bay. Izzy shuddered, hating how much this stirred him, wanting it not to stop, whimpering like a cur as Noel slid his hand up under his chin.

"Fucking hell, Peters."

"That's *Mr.* Peters to you, dolly."

"Yes sir, Mr. Peters."

"By the stars, that sounds good. What's it like to say?"

"A bit wrong, to be honest."

"Good."

At last a kiss, and like so many others it was as if it was the first and the last and the best, Izzy open completely, wanting everything, for this darkness around them and in them to become one great spell to protect them from the blinding light of hate, from cruel scrutiny and poverty and the laws of a land that if given a chance would see them both dead. If there was a woman on earth he belonged with, she was going to have her work cut out convincing him.

NOEL COULD HAVE GONE on kissing him all night, but he was no less tired than Izzy, and was due at home by daybreak. He pulled back, leaving Izzy panting, clinging to his arms, a whole different gorgeous when he was weak with desperation.

"Noel. I mean, Mr. Peters."

That elegant voice again, which shouldn't have made such a difference but which made Noel's skin tingle and his balls throb. "Yes, dolly?"

"Oh Christ..." Izzy whispered. He licked his lips, answered all in a rush. "You might not remember from earlier, sir, but I'm still waiting."

Fuck. Izzy gulped and Noel moved his hand off his throat before he throttled him out of sheer enthusiasm. "That's right. I did leave my little dolly hanging. That must mean you're damn well aching. Desperate. So desperate I could make you do anything I like." He hadn't meant to sound cruel, only to stir him a little more, but Izzy whimpered awfully as he shrank trembling into the mattress. "But I'm not going to. This is all I need."

Noel bent for another kiss, though it was never just a kiss, was always a promise they kept making to each other, to be each other's safety. He ran his hand down Izzy's bare torso, tracing the taut lines of muscle and bone, seeking, loving the leaping response of Izzy's cock. "You need more though. You deserve it. And I love it, getting you off."

"Oh, God."

"Now, now, let's not overdo it. Mr. Peters will suffice." He interrupted Izzy's snorting laugh by thrusting his hand down his drawers.

"Fuck!"

"Not tonight. You said you were tired."

"You're a hell of a wake up."

"I won't keep you then. You won't take long anyway."

"There is that," Izzy hissed, lifting his backside to shift his drawers down his hips.

"Tell me when you're going to spend."

As if Noel could miss it. As if he didn't live for this, for making Izzy squirm and pant and thrust, let Noel have his way, which at the moment was to lick then stroke then finally suck his sweet cock. There it was, the tautening of Izzy's groin, the clench of his buttocks, the helpless thrusting up into Noel's mouth.

"Oh...oh it's now..." As Noel began to stroke in time with his sucking Izzy hollered like he always did, his whole body stiffening then falling back as Noel sucked the cream right out of him. When the crisis had passed, he stretched beside him once more. Izzy could have been sleeping, breathing deeply, his voice a mere whisper.

"Sweet merciful fuck, Peters..."

"Now you don't have to change your sheets."

He breathed a little laugh. "Gimme a sec. I'll do you."

"Leave it. Go to sleep."

"Yes, sir."

"And don't make a habit of calling me that, you tart."

Noel settled against Izzy's side, his arm round his waist again. "Though you could do with someone being in charge of you. Frankly, you ain't safe on your own."

Whether Izzy agreed or not, he couldn't dispute. He had already fallen asleep.

ENOUGH

SIX MONTHS LATER

A CLEAN, QUIET ROOM. A bed big enough to share. No one to question them sharing it, for in this pitiless city they weren't the only two young men of limited means needing to double up in a room to be able to afford one at all. They still saved the best sex for the hour before or after work, when they could carry on in Izzy's suite at the bawdy, yell their heads off, which was impossible to avoid when Noel was really giving it to him.

This bed was mainly for sleeping in, though they tended to occupy it in shifts. There was the first hours after coming back from the House, when they'd collapse into exhausted slumber, often without properly undressing. Noel would force himself up as the sun rose, to head out to his family's allotment on the fringe of the city, to put in a few obligatory hours of weeding and digging, training the lad he was bringing in as his replacement.

By the time he got back, grimed and sullen, Izzy would be up, ready with tea and water for washing. Noel then got pre-eminence in the bed while Izzy read the racing forms, did his mending. Often he used the time to head up to the sports club for a go at the boxing equipment and a proper bathe.

Izzy usually made his way to the House mid-afternoon, for a tea and a chatter with the girls, keeping up with the sort of gossip that would make his job easier that evening: which clients had the morbs, who'd been barred. Happenings in government were of surprising relevance. The state of the House of Commons at five in the p.m. had a mathematical relation to the mood of Izzy's custom a few hours later. As if the toffs did it all on purpose, made a habit of crushing those beneath them in order to make their own suffering feel earned. One day Izzy would ask how much Ursula had ferreted away for him in tips from the well-to-do pricks he tormented. Perhaps it was enough to get him free.

Not that he was trapped. Only, he had no other skills of saleable use. Too slight for rough labour, not learned enough to clerk, too used to his soft life to feel much lure to any of the other opportunities granted a man of his low birth. Yes, he was valued by Ursula, and yes, it was for more than his capacity to mess someone up, but as if her word had any weight in the greater world. In the House, she was their queen. On the street, she was just another procurer, one bribe and a misstep away from ruination.

THE WEATHER THAT MORNING was filthy, sheets of rain sweeping over the rooftops, rattling the tiles inches from Izzy's head. He gave up trying to sleep, got into his clothes, and went downstairs to beg a potful of hot water off Mrs. Guild's stove. Its black enamelled body scrolled all over with coppery vines, the little Dutch-made stove was a modern marvel, with a tight-sealing chamber that burned very hot and could set a kettle boiling in a matter of minutes. In Izzy's old digs, a kind-hearted widow would have had an item of such value stolen in a twinkling. The blue and white delftware clock on her mantle too, by which he daily set his watch.

Back in their own room, he made the tea and wrapped the pot in a bit of towel to keep it hot. Aside from the creaking bed-stand, they had a cabinet that had been made for a dining room, the drawers divided into slots for knives and spoons and such. Enough space in the cupboard below for their scant possessions and whatever food they kept about, which had lead a few times to their underclothes smelling like bacon.

Not much in there today, so he'd eat on his way to work. A blooming miracle that he could make such decisions with ease, spend money almost without thinking of it. Perhaps not a miracle, for it wasn't as if Izzy hadn't earned every penny.

When he heard Noel's heavy tread on the stairs, he got out the mugs and gave them a wipe. They both liked sugar, so he broke a few bits off the hardening lump in the jar, and was just done pouring when Noel came in, soaked to the skin and moving slowly. He plopped down on the single chair, let his head fall back. Perhaps he'd slipped on the hilly paths around their garden, for he was muddy from the neck down, specks of it smeared on his shadowed cheeks.

"Tea?" Izzy said, feeling inadequate. Noel grunted, thrust out his hand without raising his head or opening his eyes. Izzy offered the handle of the mug. "It's brimming, don't spill on yourself."

"Who bleeding cares?" Noel growled. "At least I'd be warm." Still he sat up, sighing deeply as he took the first sip.

Izzy took a drink of his own, woody from having stood so long. "It's not too strong, is it? I thought you'd be back sooner."

"It's perfect."

They went on a bit without talking. In the first weeks they'd lived together, Izzy had filled these minutes with chatter. He'd taken it personally when Noel asked him to hush. He'd since learned to wait for Noel to resurface from wherever he went when he was this weary. At last his friend drained his mug, wrenched himself to his feet, then began the chore of removing his muddied clothes.

Again, Izzy wanted to help. Noel hated being helped. Instead Izzy slipped from the room and down to beg another potful from Mrs. Guild. When he got back, Noel was in his smalls, standing over the basin atop the cabinet, splashing cold water on his face. Filthy, exhausted, mumbling, he was still too gorgeous to be real, and Izzy stood a moment to calm himself. Noel hated help and hated being touched before he was ready.

He noticed Izzy, at last grinned. "What a shit of a morning."

"You looked a bit rough." Izzy came and poured a measure from Mrs. Guild's teapot into the basin, the steam spiralling.

"Mickey didn't show up. Like rain's an excuse." Noel bent to wash his face again, humming in satisfaction at the warmth of the water.

"I ought to see if I can't get you in at the sports club. Hot water for miles."

"It'd never work. They barely tolerate you as it is."

"Not so. I've got them fully hoodwinked."

Water trickling down his bare chest, Noel straightened, reached for the other towel. "You show up with someone who looks like me, they'll be asking a lot more questions than you want to be answering."

"I could pass you off as my servant—forget I said that," Izzy stammered.

"That'd be it too," Noel said, sticking out his chin. "I'd be there, minding my business, and some prick would come up and ask me where the bloody hell his tea was. Thanks, but not on your life."

"You're right," Izzy said, which was the only answer Noel tolerated. Fair enough, for no matter what hollow prejudices Izzy had survived, it was nothing compared to what got levelled at Noel, at anyone who wasn't as lily-white as Izzy himself.

Noel sighed, his whole body easing. "Sorry. I'm just choked on account of Mickey not coming through today. I hope nothing's wrong." He shivered, the autumn air finally getting to him. He got out his clean shirt from the cupboard while Izzy propped up the dormer window to tip out the basin into the convenient bit of guttering that ran along the eaves below. The rain hadn't let up, if anything was worse, pushed about by the wind so that Izzy's hands were damp by the time he was done.

Noel had got in bed, the blankets up to his chin. In another minute he'd be asleep. Izzy stretched beside him atop the covers, wanting the nearness and the smell of his skin. His friend—God help him, his love—turned towards him and Izzy leaned in and kissed that blessed cheek, not wanting to push Noel when he was this tired. But Noel moved, put his mouth under Izzy's, asking without words for a proper kiss.

What else ought a man do, except what he knows the other wants? Until Noel said no, Izzy would keep offering. He had to want this, had to love Izzy back, because this kiss was perfection. Fierce. Tongues clashing, mouths hungry, both surrendered, both pursuing, Noel pulling him back down when he would stop for breath. What else ought a man do, except give and give and take and take, as long as his strength endured?

Despite the rise of him against Izzy's front, Noel was too tired to act on his passion, and after a little he rolled away, pulling Izzy with him so his head lay on Noel's bare shoulder. "How can I miss you this much?" he murmured. "I've only been gone a few hours."

"Come to work early."

Noel's chesty laugh rumbled. "Don't want to alarm Mrs. Guild?"

"Or break the bed, get arrested. You know, the usual."

They kissed once more, but Noel was fading, his lips slack, his sighs softening. At last his head fell back, his arms merely resting on Izzy. "I'll dream of you," he murmured,

his eyes fluttering closed.
"You damn well better."

OBLIGATIONS

WHEN NOEL WOKE, THE rain had stopped and a soggy sun was doing its best to steam through the clouds. Their room caught a good amount of daylight, and he lay for a while basking in the accumulated warmth of the blankets, for the air was hardly warm to judge from the chilled tip of his nose.

Izzy was gone, as expected. On the single chair, he'd left a neatly folded stack of clothes. Noel's, back from the launderers, which meant Izzy had gathered up the mud-caked apparel from the morning, taken it downstairs, brought up the clean lot and laid it out. Noel's boots stood beside the door, damp from sponging but perfectly wearable.

He laid back and stared at the ceiling a little longer. What was it about Izzy's care that was so humiliating? Other that it suggested his friend thought him incompetent. He knew that had nothing to do with it. Izzy was if anything in awe of Noel's stamina, his willingness to push himself when other people required it.

No one had ever expected anything different of Noel. Born last to a hard working family, he'd been ever underfoot, fed and petted but mainly ignored until he was old enough to be of use. From then on, he'd worked. Hence the twinge of guilt when Izzy showed unasked attention to his needs. He wasn't meant to need a thing. Little Noelly, bringing up the rear, catching grasshoppers to save the cabbages for market.

By comparison, this life was proper luxurious. Peace and quiet, a soft bed and someone to warm it, endless little kindnesses between them. Very few secrets. The work was tolerable, at times enjoyable. His parents had come to terms with his commitments to Ursula, mainly as they believed he'd never take it further than tending bar.

He had to give that lad Mickey a right talking to. First a question, to be sure of why he'd not shown up at the plot today. If it was mere reluctance, Noel would threaten to sack him. He had no patience for shirkers. No time either, for he couldn't keep this routine much longer, working two wholly separate and contradictory jobs. Ursula's demands were only getting more demanding.

Thinking of her made him think again of Izzy, of his ask for Noel to come in early to work. So they could take their time, make the most of each other. In three throbbing heartbeats, he was thick with want, and like his hands belonged to someone else (he knew exactly who) he fumbled open his drawers. Urgently grasped himself, hissing through his teeth at his own barbarity. Yet he'd have so much more enjoyment later if he waited now. He stopped, stared at the ceiling and thought about trowels and turnips until he calmed. Then he got up, dressed in the garb Izzy had laid out for him, and left for the night.

THE HOUSE WAS QUIET this early in the afternoon, and
Noel had the dressing room to himself. First off, a proper
bath. This was one luxury Izzy couldn't provide, though
the House had only a copper tub and a pair of buckets
behind a screen in the corner. Daring of Izzy to think that
Noel might be granted access to the sports club's facilities. Its rarefied membership were precisely the types who
would never see past Noel's colour. Men whose fortunes
had been made in large part by their recent ancestors having owned his.

He finished as the staff started to arrive. This many
months into what they all called his apprenticeship, he'd
lost his modesty around the girls, and while drying off he
chatted over the screen with Prue as she took the curling papers out of her henna-rouged hair. Wrapped in the
thick dressing gown he'd gifted himself, he went up to the
suite. He got his evening wear out of the wardrobe and
was brushing clean the tailcoat when Izzy arrived, cheeks
flushed from the hot baths at the club, his wet hair in
shining curls. Izzy hated looking young and normally kept
his hair brushed back and oiled into submission, but Noel
found him perfect as he was.

Though Noel expected him to come right up and kiss
him, waste no time, Izzy was moving slow, easing out of
his jacket like his shoulders hurt. "I might have overdone
it."

"Were you boxing?"

Izzy sat on the bed, flexing his hand. "It just felt so good to punch something." He laid back, arms cast over his head, eyes closed.

Despite the heat rising from his groin, Noel shivered, hurt by his friend's hurt. He moved to the bedside by Izzy's head. Izzy opened his eyes and gazed up at him. Grinned crookedly. "I can see straight up your nostrils from here."

Noel snorted a laugh. "You cunt. Here I am, feeling sympathetic."

"Oh, I'm a cunt, am I?"

"Yeah. And you know what happens to cunts, don't you?"

Izzy licked his lips, his eyes flashing. Noel shivered again, this time from that internal heat. He doffed the dressing gown and tossed it at the chair, not caring that he missed, then knelt on the bed overtop Izzy's head, intending to make good use of that insolent mouth of his. Paused at the solid thump of Ursula's walking stick knocking on the door. For no one else on earth would he stop. But if she was interrupting, there had to be good cause.

"Mr. Pound, Mr. Peters," she called through the door, "I'm afraid you're needed in the salon immediately. I'll grant you two minutes. And please dress your best. Our client's satisfaction is of the utmost importance."

ROSES

HIS HEAD SINGING, HIS trousers pinching his unsatisfied cock with every step, Izzy was glad of the whiskey Sal gave him as soon as they got in the salon. Near everyone was there, dressed for top brass. Even Ursula, wearing a low-shouldered grey dress, her icy beauty near unearthly, despite her keeping her forearms clamped to her sides as if in constant fear of the garment falling off.

Marisol swanned in at the end in a flurry of green feathers and swagged skirts, ever conscious of her elevated status, though what her privilege was founded on Izzy had yet to learn. Ursula waved her near and handed her a thick envelope. Marisol took one look and offered it back. "Burn this one too."

"I really think you ought to open at least one of these letters. They're from a solicitor's office."

"You want to open it? Be my guest," Marisol drawled. She stuck the corner of the envelope in Ursula's décolletage and sauntered off to pour herself a drink.

Her lips twitching, Ursula took the offending envelope from her top and popped off the fancy seal to take out a thick fold of papers. She scanned the first, her face going impossibly paler. "Mari, you really ought to read this."

"Ugh, fine." Carrying a very full wine glass, Marisol strolled back, rolling her painted eyes as she took the letter. At first she quit sneering. Then she got very still, so still everyone in the room noticed for to see Marisol back-footed was a rarity and quite disconcerting.

"I...am going now," she mumbled to no one in particular. Then she turned and walked out without once looking up from the letter.

"I suppose we can get by without her," Ursula said with a grimace. "As for the rest of us, we've a two-hour reservation to start the evening. After which, normal business will resume."

"A reservation? For the whole lot of us?" Honey asked, hand on her hip.

"An exclusive reservation for the House entire. It is of the utmost importance that the identity of our client be known to as few people as possible."

"Must be a big un." Honey waggled her eyebrows, earning a chuckle from the room.

"There are few bigger," Ursula replied, her voice trembling in a way Izzy had never heard.

"Is that so?" Honey said with much less confidence, as the rest quieted.

Ursula took the leather-bound ledger from under her arm and held it before her like she was about to lead a hymn. "I do hope you'll forgive me for these rather exacting specifications. To say we cannot afford to disappoint this client is a grave understatement. Here, therefore, are our requirements." She opened the ledger and began to read.

THE SALON WAS JUST broad enough that, elbow to elbow, they could stand all in a line. No one was to speak, to raise their eyes, to move from their pose, the women's hands clasped before them, the men's behind. Noel was some ways along, closer to the door, and Izzy was about to dare a glimpse when the salon door opened.

He looked down, focusing on the carpet and its pattern of blowsy roses. After a bit, a man's black trousers came into view atop a pair of highly polished shoes. The trousers passed by, and Izzy realized he was holding his breath waiting for Ursula's skirts to follow.

This never happened. Instead, the man made it to the end of the row and started back, passing behind them. Izzy curled his toes, fighting a very strong urge to step forward, turn around, not get sneaked up on. More than his job was worth, possibly his life, and he went back to staring at the roses, pale pink in a dark green carpet, the colours blurred by countless feet.

"This one," said the man, standing very near. Izzy stiffened his back. Looked at the lovely roses. "And this one," the same cultured voice said from further down.

"Very good, Mr. Everley," Ursula replied from near the door.

"Your people will have ten minutes."

"Yes, Mr. Everley." The door opened and closed. Ursula

sighed, her skirts swishing. "All right, everyone. You can pass the time downstairs. All except you, of course. And you, Mr. Pound."

It hit like a punch to Izzy's guts, the whiskey suddenly afire. This was more than he wanted, more honour than he needed, a task beyond him if that task was to anoint some royal brat with a horsewhip. The others filed out, those nearest murmuring condolences, as if he was on his way to a funeral.

"Ah shit."

Izzy looked up. Besides Ursula, the only one left in the room was Noel.

"Fucking hell!"

"I'm sorry," Noel stammered.

"You're sorry? Why the hell were you even in that line-up? You can't have this be your first job." Izzy drew breath, preparing to tell Ursula off, but Noel spoke first.

"It won't be."

"It what?"

Noel cleared his throat. "He's not the first."

"And when did this happen?" Izzy demanded, feeling hot and very stupid.

Noel shrugged, glanced at Ursula, silent by the door. "Few weeks ago. I didn't tell you because I knew you'd try and get involved."

"Of bleeding course I would! What were you thinking?"

"You can't keep protecting me. I'm a grown man, Pound. It's up to me what happens."

"But...fucking hell." There was an armchair in front of Izzy and he fell into it, heart shuddering.

"I'll ensure the room is prepared," Ursula murmured.

The door clicked shut behind her but Izzy didn't move. Noel's legs appeared, then he crouched down to look him in the face.

"I'm sorry."

"You gotta stop saying that," Izzy croaked, furious at the tears trying to spring up.

"It was too strange, getting you involved. I didn't want you watching if I couldn't hack it."

"I wouldn't have minded."

"It's not always about you. I mean it is but...shit." Noel looked down, biting his lips, and the sight of him suffering was worse than discovering he'd kept this secret.

"Forget it. I'll not hold it against you. I couldn't. You only wanted to spare me."

"I did," Noel said, his voice cracking. "I wanted it to have nothing to do with you. So you wouldn't be thinking about it, after."

"Never. You're a thing unto yourself, you are. Now, let's go and find out what this regal prick wants from us."

Smiling at last, Noel stood and offered his hand. Izzy got up, but didn't let go.

"One last thing, before we get into it..."

"Yeah?"

It took doing, to ask for something meaningless. "Might I have a kiss?"

Noel smiled, simply radiant. "You say that like I wouldn't want to."

"One doesn't like to presume."

There was reluctance, and then there was the pleasure of holding out, waiting for Noel's touch on his cheek, his thumb tracing Izzy's jaw to end at his chin, tip his head back. Despite the swooning spin of the earth beneath his feet, Izzy kept his eyes open, craving this sight as much as any sensation, Noel gazing at him in rapt contemplation, as if he'd never seen anything more delightful.

It was a kiss to end all kisses, Noel consuming him, pinning Izzy's head between his strong hands. Making love with their mouths, until both were panting, clinging to each other, nearly falling. Enough of a kiss to last through whatever awaited them. At least they would face it together.

His Highness

With everyone else downstairs, Noel found the house unpleasantly quiet. Ursula was waiting at the open door of the Imperial suite. Of course. No one else was inside, and she shut the door then came to meddle with their jackets and hair.

"I'm so sorry about this, gentlemen."

"I am well tired of hearing that word," Izzy muttered, tipping his head for her to adjust his collar.

"Are we not to know anything about him?" Noel asked, shaking out his tingling hands. "How are we even meant to address him? As we would ordinarily? Or do we call him Your Grace or something?"

"That's for dukes, innit?" Izzy said, beginning to fidget, toes tapping, hands plucking at his trouser out-seams as Ursula fussed.

"You ought not to have to address the client at all," she said. "He's only here to watch."

"Thank Christ," Izzy said. She finished and let him go

and he stepped back, rubbing at his neck. "Because I was not excited about smacking around someone so far above us you can't even tell us his title."

"Right? He wouldn't even need to get you done for a crime. Just, whop," Noel said, miming the swing of the axe. "There's your head on a pike."

Ursula gave them what Noel thought of as her motherly look. "Come, now. It's not the time of the Tudors." Someone knocked on the door, interrupting whatever else she might have said.

"Lord help me, I'm sick of hearing that," Izzy groaned. Ursula flashed him double the look. He stiffened his back, hands clasped behind. "Don't mind me, ma'am. Just regretting all my choices in life," he added in a murmur only Noel heard as Ursula started for the door.

She opened it for a porcelain-skinned man dressed in impeccable eveningwear. Noel looked down as instructed. "At ease, boys," Ursula said, her voice taut. "The secretary Mr. Everley has some last instructions for you."

Not gentlemen. Boys. By God, the fee on this had better be tremendous. Noel's avarice made his own stomach roil. What kind of man was he becoming?

Mr. Everley completed his circling inspection and stopped beside Ursula. "They'll do. Assuming they perform as expected. Don't disappoint us."

All of it said to their procurer, as if they weren't standing right there. As if they were toys to be wound up with a key and set running. Beside him, Izzy was trembling, from rage or terror or both. Noel took a deep breath, then another, hoping to lead Izzy, cool him off.

Ursula and Everley ended their muttered conversation.

She looked ghostly, all colour washed from her already pale cheeks, too much of her snowy bosom showing, her low-cut dress seeming borrowed from another body, so different was it from her typical mannish jackets. Pursing her lips, she curtseyed ever so slightly to Everley and left the room without another glance their way.

As the door clicked shut behind her, the slightest of moans slipped past Izzy's closed lips. Everley turned to them, his face a blank, right down to his glassy grey eyes.

"Which one of you is the sissy?" he said, the word more distressing than usual when pronounced so impeccably.

Noel glanced at Izzy, whose cheeks were blazing pink, giving the game away on the instant. Everley smiled, or at least spread his lips enough to conform to the basic notion.

"As I thought. You needn't hold back," he said, addressing Noel. "There's very little his highness hasn't seen. Or done. You have five minutes to collect yourselves." With that Everley turned on his sharp heel and left the room.

"His highness..." Izzy breathed.

"He didn't have to say that. Call you that."

Izzy shrugged as he tried to muster up his old smirk. "Yeah, well, we all know I'm the wife in this little domestic drama of ours."

"I'm sorry."

"Fucking hell, another thing I'm getting sick of hearing." Izzy stomped over to the decanters on the sideboard and poured a measure. He raised it, paused, set it down hard without taking a drink, his whole body rigid with inexpressible emotion. Conscious of the passing seconds, Noel went to him, pulled him around, pulled his stiff frame into an embrace. Held him until he softened, responded, put his arms around Noel, pressed his lips against Noel's soft throat.

"One more kiss," Izzy murmured.

"Always."

To kiss him was as good as it ever was, even tinged with fear, even knowing this was the last kindness that might pass between them for hours. Kissing Izzy made all else go away, the poverty and perfidy and deadly scrutiny that haunted two such desperate souls as them. In this moment, in Izzy's arms, their hearts were indivisible, beating in time, against all odds.

At last they stood panting, foreheads together, immersed in each other's protection. "Do us a favour?" Izzy murmured.

"Of course."

He raised his head, tears clinging to his dark lashes. "Don't kiss me in front of him. Not like this."

"No. This is just for us."

"And don't say my name. Or Mr. Pound."

"What am I meant to call you?"

He managed a smile. "Whatever you like. Cocksucker, trollop."

"Scum?"

Izzy laughed, a bitter rasp, so utterly unlike him that Noel shivered. "That'll do."

At the rattle of the door handle they sprung apart to stand as they had before, side by side, their hands clasped behind their backs, their eyes committedly on the carpet. Noel had half expected a master of ceremonies, a bugle salute, a suite of retainers, but it was only Everley, followed by a matching pair of shoes and legs which stopped before them.

"Well done, Everley," the client said in purring tones. "This should be quite good sport."

"Thank you, sir. Your usual seat is prepared."

The second set of legs departed. Everley spoke to them low and quick. "Do you understand what's expected?"

Summoning every ounce of mastery he'd earned, Noel raised his head to address the secretary. "I would like to know what you meant precisely by *don't hold back*. I'm not versed in all this upper class speak, me. I'd like to know in plain English."

Everley's blank expression remained. "It means you are to beat him. The harder the better. Is that sufficiently plain?"

"Yes, sir."

IF IZZY WAS SHAMMING, he was magnificent, could have stormed any stage in the land. He howled and sobbed, writhing under the blows, head lolling between rounds. Noel went until his head was spinning with rage, with the punch of the brandy, with sheer exhaustion of body and soul. Until Izzy's thighs and buttocks were a ruin of wicked bruises and red welts and his shoulders heaved with his sobbing breath. As Everley approached Noel fell back. The secretary looked hard at him, and he took the hint and further lowered his gaze as the client stepped up to Izzy and did something that made him cry out in genuine alarm.

You've got a weapon. Noel forced his grip to loosen on

the cane. He was not going to beat a leader of the nation to death with a stick. The man chuckled, a deep and dirty sound that made Noel feel queasy.

"Good enough. We'll pay."

Which meant there'd been a chance they wouldn't. Noel's whole arm shook with the effort not to strike. This was exploitation, plain and simple. This was what privilege was made for.

They left, at last. As the door clicked shut, Noel threw aside the cane and hastened to Izzy, began unbuckling the ankle straps that bound him to the whipping frame.

"Is it over?" Izzy rasped. "Are they gone?"

"Yeah."

"Bloody hell goddamn mother of fucking mercy sweet Christ that fucking hurt!" What started as a mutter ended on a yell that left Noel's ears ringing.

"Say it again," he chuckled, standing up to reach the straps around Izzy's wrists. "Scotland didn't quite hear you."

"Fuck Scotland. No, fuck the aristocracy. The lot of them can rot."

"Steady, he might still be in the building."

"I fucking do not care. And for the love of God, hurry. I've got to piss so bad I can taste it."

A Free Man

It was humiliating how quickly he recovered. That meant he was getting too used to brutality. More than once in the week that followed, Izzy had to give a client a slap for eyeing his bruises too boldly. *And you thought I was a fright,* he'd snarl. *Imagine, there's a man out there that can top even me.*

They'd apparently all left enormous tips. He was going to ask today how much Ursula was holding for him. He'd not wanted to take home more than his base wage while living with his family. Too much dosh and they'd have gotten used to it, cursed him whenever he fell short. It was going on two years that Izzy had worked for Ursula, who would have marked down every penny he'd made in one of her ledgers. An honest whoremonger: would wonders never cease?

He scuffed along the sidewalk, lost in thought, dry beech leaves cluttering past his feet, another sign of the season's passing. He hoped his and Noel's little room could be kept warm when the winter came, perhaps by hanging a quilt over the window. If not, maybe Ursula would relent, grant him a room on a more permanent basis. He had to be a special case. Noel as well. Now that he was staff.

Out of everything Izzy regretted about the Royal Pain in the Arse, as they'd been referring to their client, what he hated most was learning that Noel had kept a secret from him. And such a secret, the kind that could change everything. Which of course it had.

There was nothing left in Izzy's life that wasn't this life. Not a friend he could count on, a haven to run to, a coin in his pocket that wasn't intimately tied to the fact of how he made those coins. The worst thing he might discover from Ursula was that the money she'd put aside wasn't worth the effort he'd expended. The risks he ran, the men he tolerated. The crime he committed again and again, and for which only he would be punished.

Fine sentiments when on his way to commit that very crime. Stomping more than was polite, he was coming up on the alley when the royal pain's secretary Mr Everley emerged from a flash four-in-hand stopped at the curb ahead.

Briefly, Izzy thought about running in the opposite direction. The big carriage was too cumbersome to catch up with a terrified man on foot. Everley didn't seem like the sort to debase himself by sprinting through the streets. But they'd only come back tomorrow, angry for being made to wait.

He stopped and regarded Everley from a respectful distance. "Am I meant to get in?"

"What do you think?" the secretary replied in the same

snobbish tone as always.

That I bleeding well ought to have run. Having no choice to speak of, Izzy forced himself the last few steps and climbed into the closed vehicle, despising the servile instinct that made him take off his hat as he did so.

And there he was, exactly who Izzy had guessed the unseen client to be, exactly who he had prayed and prayed for it not to be. "Oh, sweet Jesus."

"Your highness will be quite sufficient," the unctuous voice purred from the corner of the lushly upholstered carriage. He looked very much like his portraits, was dressed as he ought to be, in sublimely cut black gabardine, with silk lapels and shiny boots and one of those sashes across his waistcoat as if the shit had just come from the palace.

If Izzy was lucky, he'd insult the man enough to get killed. Because every alternative seemed much, much worse, as the royal pain tapped the place beside him to indicate where Izzy should sit. Which he did, because what else could he do?

Everley didn't get in, the dip of the vehicle suggesting he'd climbed up with the driver. The carriage stayed otherwise still. A sliver of hope, that Izzy wasn't being carted away. A sliver which crumbled under the heavy weight of the man's hand on Izzy's thigh.

"Ezekiel Pound. Son of Morris and Petunia, of Horlick Close, Whitechapel. Shall I name your brothers?"

"No, your h-h-highness."

"You understand your situation?"

"Unfortunately."

"Fate is a cruel mistress, Ezekiel, is she not?" The man squeezed Izzy's thigh firmly, and he whimpered despite himself. The man licked his lips, slid his hand to the inside of Izzy's leg and squeezed harder. Izzy moaned again, now cried out as the man pinched him on his inner thigh, using his manicured nails, then twisting.

Any other man, Izzy would have belted across the side of the head, then again for good measure, for taking such license. By murphy, he'd not have even gotten into another man's carriage. Not Morrison or Sir Carey or even that bloody duke, who always blubbed then paid double. Here was a man who could destroy every single one of them with a wave of his hand. Not only Izzy and Ursula but Kentley and Morwell and the duke, all in one. All of that power concentrated behind this groomed countenance, these fine clothes, this pointlessly sadistic touch that went on and on and was going to tear a hole in his thigh in a moment—

The man released him and he collapsed back against the seat, pressing his hand against the throbbing point. No escape, as the man grabbed Izzy's wrist and dragged him near, then hoisted him up to straddle his lap.

The bugger was stronger than expected for a man who had never had to work a day in his life. Fabric tore—Izzy's trouser seat? His shirt? The least of his worries as the man grabbed him by the throat, his thumb and forefinger placed to either side just so, right where Izzy himself might, if he wanted a client to come over all faint. With his other hand, the man held Izzy's arm behind his back, the ache in his shoulder yet one more agony as the man began to close his hand round Izzy's neck.

This was how he died.

They'd find him in the alley, bruised and scarred and

damn well dead. Because he'd been too stupid to run for his life. Noel would find him and—

Noel deserved better. If Izzy succumbed, Noel would be next. Better that Izzy died trying to warn his friend, his love, his only hope, than to leave him prey to this same despicable fate.

If he lived long enough to get free. Already his head was swimming. He jerked back and the pressure eased, the man's legs wobbling under Izzy's as he attempted too much torment at once. Bleeding amateur. Izzy squirmed again and the man's grip loosened, his fierce grin fading. He wasn't used to being disobeyed.

Ezekiel Pound was no man's slave. He was a free man, owing nothing to the nation which had granted nothing to him. Neither kindness nor care, not safety nor feeding nor shelter, nothing but the ground on which to be born and die, and whatever he and his kin could steal from men like this.

If this was how he died, he'd die fighting. The man still had a hand on his throat, nails digging in as he lost his grip. Izzy wrenched himself back and forth, ignoring the pain of his arm pinioned behind him. His knees found the carriage seat: leverage at last, and with an almighty twist he tore away from the man's grip.

He found himself on his arse on the floor, the man gaping at him stupidly. If the carriage door was locked, Izzy never knew, for rather than fiddle with the latch he put his heels together and slammed them against the door. A second blow and it swung wild, a cry from outside suggesting he'd struck Everley. No less than the devil deserved, another thing he'd not stop to discover, as he leapfrogged out the door and took off at double top speed, faster than he'd ever run or hoped to do again.

He'd left his hat. Better, for they'd recognize him less. His boldly checked jacket held only coins and his new handkerchief, and after a few wild turns he slowed enough to strip it off and toss it into the next alley he passed. Someone would appreciate the find. All that mattered to Izzy was surviving long enough to see Noel again.

JUST A KISS

NO SAFE PLACES. NOWHERE he could go where he wasn't known. The royal pain knew his parents' address. Would kill them out of nothing but spite. And Izzy was such a heartless shit that he'd let it happen.

The worst was not knowing who counted as an enemy. A royal had such reach, anyone Izzy passed might have been on the take. Of those who weren't, none were immune to being bribed or bullied into compliance by a man of that rarefied privilege.

The wretched rain was back, turning the gutters to filthy streams and the potholes to puddles and soaking Izzy to the skin by the time he made it home via every alleyway he could string together. He'd lost his key to the front door somewhere in his escape, and as he came along the alley behind his building he once again patted his wet waistcoat pocket where the key to Ursula's was firmly fixed to its little chain. Any port in a storm. But he so very much wished to get home, one last time.

He had thought through every possible solution, and he kept coming back to the one. The simplest solution, the one that would least disrupt everyone else's lives. Noel would hate it. Poor cobber didn't have a choice.

Pointlessly wiping the rain from his face for the hundredth time, Izzy crept up the narrow lane between his building and its neighbour. At the footpath he paused, silently cursing the gloom of cloud and the rain trickling from his lank hair into his eyes, blurring the world into undifferentiated grey. He wiped his face again, then backed silently away from the street, unnerved by what he couldn't have said, some fine sense honed by years of living on the edge of many an abyss.

He retreated all the way to the alley. Three storeys up, the dormer window in his flat projected from the peaked roof. As he watched, a pigeon settled with its fellows along the ridge. Lucky little pricks. Another one fluttered down beside and Izzy looked further up. The drop from the next building's roof to his was no more than six or seven feet. Not a soul would see him coming, besides the birds. He began to backtrack along the alley, hoping for something to climb.

Several dirty, tedious, terrifying minutes later, after scaling a brick wall, dodging the dog in the subsequent yard, clambering over a shed then up the shaky balconies of hopefully oblivious tenants, and the worst of all, when he'd found the distance from the upper roof to the lower was rather more like ten feet than six, he was perched on the peak of his window. His right ankle smarted from the drop, the noise of which had likely given Noel a fright. Izzy had certainly given himself one, for a wrong move and he'd have missed the narrow bit of reasonably flat roof and slid right off. As it was he only hurt one ankle and bruised his knees, though that wasn't making it any easier to clamber about.

Noel might not even be home. Then Izzy would have to break in. Was that a crime at one's own residence? He inched forward, hands slipping on the slate tiles. He hadn't thought this part through. He was on top of the window, but he had to get below it, knock, get Noel's attention...

A gust of wind pushed at him, blattering rain in his face and threatening to tear him from his perch. Hunching against the roof ridge, he sobbed once, caught his breath. He hadn't the time to dwell on how royally fucked he was. If he didn't get inside, he'd die of plain old gravity. Doing his utmost not to look past the roof to the very distant ground, he slipped his leg over so he crouched to one side of the dormer peak. Inch by inch, he crept sideways, at last reached the dormer face.

Two feet of roof extended below the windowsill before the poorly attached guttering began. One hand on the dormer, he moved as close to the roof edge as he dared. He was reaching his free hand around to tap on the glass when the window creaked up. A second later, a steaming stream emerged: Noel, pissing out the window into the eaves trough, as they did more often than not.

As the arc diminished, Izzy whistled, the short, sharp sound they'd picked as an alarm. He did it again, and a third time as Noel finished. Izzy shifted down one more inch, his shoes sliding on the slate. He whistled once more and a brown nap of hair projected into his line of sight.

"Peters," he hissed, too cold and terrified to make much

of a sound. "For fuck's sake, Noel."

Noel's whole head emerged. "Saints preserve us, Pound. What are you doing out there?"

"Ask me again in a minute. First, save my life?"

IT TOOK SOME DOING, and more than once Noel's heart leapt into his throat, but he managed to haul Izzy in through the window. Noel was glad he'd dallied at home rather than striking out for Ursula's early, pushing away the thought of what would have become of Izzy otherwise as he went to ask Mrs. Guild to put on the kettle.

When he got back to their room, Izzy was still crouched on the rug like a sodden cat. He'd lost his jacket and hat, the rest of his clothes as soaked as Noel's after a rainy morning in the market plot. When he didn't move, Noel got down by him, touched his shoulder. The contact broke through some barrier, and Izzy went from catatonic to grabbing Noel and pulling him close for a kiss of unparalleled passion.

Questions could wait. Izzy needed this. Noel could taste it, knew this was Izzy's way of overcoming fear, by having it fucked out of him. They were in each other's laps, Izzy's clothes soaking Noel's, but when Noel slipped his hand from Izzy's damp cheek to his neck, his friend stiffened, half pulling away. Noel bent to look, saw the scrape of nails and the red marks by the pressure points. Right where Ursula had taught him, when you wanted to...

"Who did this to you?" Izzy didn't answer, dropping his head, whimpering when Noel tried to raise his chin. "If I guess will you admit it? Was it RPA?"

"He was going to kill me," Izzy breathed, his head butted against Noel's chest, hands knotted in Noel's damp shirt front. "Like I was nothing at all."

"It's all right—"

"It's not all right," Izzy blurted. He looked up, tears streaming down his bloodless cheeks. "He'll kill me for sure now. Why the fuck did I run? Why the fuck did I ever start this life? Why the fuck anything? Jesus, Noel...if not for you...I'm so sorry. I'm sorry I made this your life."

"You're sorry? I thought you hated that word." The wrong tone, as Izzy's face pinched in anger. "Forget it," Noel said quickly. "I didn't mean nothing but to cheer you up. Apologize all you want."

With a sob that was nearly a laugh, Izzy chose instead to kiss him. He yanked Noel hard towards him, so that they were suddenly laying down in a tangle of wet clothes and limbs. In danger of knocking his head on the leg of the bed, Noel rolled the other way, ending on his back. Izzy was atop him, and he scrambled back to straddle Noel's legs and get his hand on his trouser front.

"You don't have to—"

"Yes I bleeding well do." He'd already got Noel's fly unbuttoned. Noel shrugged his braces off his shoulders to oblige his friend in undressing him, before something got damaged. Like Noel himself as Izzy gripped him too hard through the gap in his clothes.

"Easy," he grunted. "You don't want to break that off before I get a chance to use it on you."

Hallelujah for Izzy's crooked grin, as he let go and settled back on his heels, the panic ebbing. "Don't mind me. Just,

I never thought I'd see him again."

"Who?"

"Little Noelly," he said, glancing towards Noel's stand, which was pushing up his cotton drawers through his open trousers like a sail in a black cloth sea, though the sound of his family nickname set the sail to lowering.

"Bloody hell, Pound. My parents call me that."

Izzy snorted, though he had the grace not to laugh out loud. "So they do. Never mind. It don't change how I feel about him. Or you. This is why I fought, though. This is why I ran."

He'd come over all serious, his eyes brightly focused, his smirk a mere suggestion. Noel felt that fluttering inside, like Izzy's feelings were something to fear.

"I'm that good a shag, am I?" he quipped. He regretted his irreverence as Izzy barked another bitter laugh.

"You're everything."

"I'm not."

"Sure feels like you are. Isn't that enough, feeling it?" He shifted nearer, his hands on Noel's hips. "Isn't that how it's meant to be when you love someone?"

"That's what this is, isn't it?"

"Gotta be. I thought I was going to die. And all that mattered was that I kept him from hurting you." Any second Izzy was sure to start bawling again, waste time they didn't have, shed tears that changed nothing. Praying he wasn't ruining the fragile moment, Noel grabbed Izzy's arms, pulled his love close and kissed him as if this was the last kiss they'd ever have. Just a kiss though, both of them sensible enough to not truly wish to ball in wet clothes on the dirty floor of a place they only hoped was safe, though

Izzy stayed atop him, wrapped in Noel's arms, his head on Noel's chest.

"Imagine," Izzy murmured after a little. "If I weren't a man."

"How would that help?"

"I'd marry you. I'm serious," he said as Noel chuckled.

"We'd still be skint."

"True, but I'd not expect my dear husband to support me. I'd not even have to change jobs."

"I might have to."

"Nah, we'd gin it up to a real act. Watch 'em ball for a shilling, or get in on the act for a bob."

Noel laughed again. "They pay to do that already."

Izzy squirmed and Noel let him sit up. He drew breath like he wanted to speak. Noel found he was holding his own breath, waiting, but Izzy only smiled.

"Fucking hell, am I ever glad to see you."

EASY

NOEL HAD TO ARGUE Izzy into coming to work. He didn't want to be alone, but he was terrified of being seen. It was the need to ask Ursula about his gratuities which convinced him. Making do with what was about the flat, Izzy dressed in Noel's clothes and dotted his blanched face with candle ash like he had either freckles or pox or both, though Noel balked at the suggestion that they cut Izzy's curling hair.

"With what?" Noel asked, looking around their more or less empty flat.

"Haven't you got a pen knife?"

"I'm to use a pen knife to cut your hair? You've gone round the bend."

"So would you, with what I've had happen," Izzy said crossly, turning up his jacket collar.

"You can wear my good hat," Noel said, taking it from its nail on the wall and passing it to him. "I'll wear your old one. And we might as well get on, she'll be losing her mind as it is, wondering where we are."

The newish bowler was a little too large for Izzy and sat low on his head. He pulled it down to his eyebrows. "Bet you anything Everley went straight to her," he muttered.

"Regardless, she'd not give you up," Noel said, unlocking the door.

"Like she'd have a choice."

Tucking his chin into his collar, Izzy followed him out, waiting for Noel to case the stairwell before moving an inch from the door. Downstairs, it was another argument to convince Izzy to wear the expense of a cab, to get to the House as swiftly as possible, though Noel agreed to disembark at the far end of Spencer Street.

Hunched against the blatting rain, they were just two dark forms among many hastening along the dreary street. Though they both kept watch for regal carriages and blank faced secretaries, they reached the narrow alley without incident, slipped along and so inside the House through the staff entrance.

Light, warmth, the smell of perfume and the sound of women's laughter: the comforts of home. Noel would have gone to Ursula's office, but Izzy turned the other way and headed to their room.

Fair enough, for they were both soggy and could do with refreshing before they ruined Ursula's life. Noel followed him in and closed the door. Was suddenly flat against it, pushed there by Izzy, whose mouth met his with frightened urgency. Fair turn again, for a kiss could always calm him, but Noel's response only drove Izzy harder, his touch frantic as he tried to unbutton Noel's shirt and trousers at the same time, kissing his mouth, his face, his neck.

"We're already late," Noel gasped as soon as he had air.

"Don't care," Izzy murmured against the hollow behind Noel's ear.

"We ought to tell her what happened to you."

Izzy pulled back with a grimace. "I really was hoping to forget about that for a little. And don't you dare say sorry," he added as Noel opened his mouth. "I know full well what she's going to say, and neither of us wants to hear it. Just let me live in this dream of mine a bit longer. One more hour."

"We don't have an hour."

There, that smirk. "Fine, twenty minutes, then. Please."

If Noel spoke again, he'd only say something else stupid or painful, make another joke out of Izzy's heartache and his own. So he nodded, and Izzy smiled, and he was so bloody beautiful and it was perfect and still awful and Noel felt all the way down to his toes the need to fuck to make the noise in his head go away.

Starting with this kiss, frightening in its intensity, like Izzy was drowning and Noel was his rescue. Maybe it was the other way round, as Izzy lead him step by stumbling step to the bed, their arms locked around each other. Next to undress, and damn the time, Noel would bare every inch of Izzy's skin then cover it with kisses.

Agreement, not in words but in the desperation of Izzy's hands, to make them both the same, as much as ever they were: both men, both naked as God had made them. That was part of why he loved Izzy, for his having made no matter of their outer differences, for seeing straight to Noel's soul.

They lay entwined in bed, face to face, Izzy's leg up over

Noel's hip, Noel's cock sliding beneath his arse. "Tell me, in this dream of yours what happens next?" he asked.

"In my dream? You fuck me. You spread me and fill me and don't let up until you're done."

A wave of dizzying desire passed over Noel, followed by a flush of hot guilt. "All things considered, I'd have thought that's the last thing you'd want."

"But it's you doing it. No one else gets to do that to me, not anymore. Not for anything." Izzy stopped squirming, looked at Noel squarely, seeming to have come to some resolution. "And no one ever will again. I swear."

There was that flutter in Noel's chest again, and a taste in the air that was like danger but not. "Don't be daft, Pound."

"I want to be daft. I want to promise you something spectacular. If I could, honour bright, I'd give you all of me. Make you marry me, so I could pledge in front of God and all the world that I love you. But I can't, so let me give you this. Let me swear that there's only space for you in my heart."

"It ain't your heart we were talking about." He slid his hand down the curve of Izzy's arse, making him groan and pivot against him.

"Then why is it, whenever you touch me there, I want to yell *I love you*?"

The feeling in Noel's chest was no longer a flutter but a hurricane. "Say that again," he murmured, shocked that he hadn't shouted.

"Then why is it, whenever—" Izzy started, his eyes darting as he tried to remember the wording.

Noel stopped him with a laugh. "I just meant the last

bit."

Izzy looked at him squarely, one eyebrow raised. "I love you?"

"Yeah. Except not as a question."

"I love you."

This time he said it simply, as if the words passed back and forth between them all the time, but for all that Noel felt, to claim in in that way was something else entire. And he was meant to say it back.

He felt it, that he loved this darling scoundrel in his arms, with a fierceness he'd never known. He opened his mouth, his stiff tongue unable to loose the wild storm in his heart. "Why is it so frightening to say?" he mumbled.

Izzy chuckled, not unkindly. "I been saying it in my head for months. Try saying it to yourself a few times. Get used to the sound."

Noel closed his eyes, thinking back to any time he'd heard the words. One was meant to live in God's love, but it seemed a shabby and irregular embrace, to judge from the moral deficit of the upper classes and the cruelties heaped on the lower. His parents didn't speak of love, his sisters only in terms of what they'd never find. Ballads, poems, stage plays, all of which were false.

But there were feelings and then there were the words you had available, which could never equal each other. Hence all that poetry, thousands of words and none giving more than a glimpse. Three little words were enough, a spell to cast on oneself and the object of one's affection. A spell you kept having to cast, in case it wore off. He'd been almost a year with Izzy and he wasn't planning on wearing off.

I love you. He thought it again, imagining the words written on a pristine page. *I love you, Ezekiel Pound.* Daring, charming, tempting, endangered, ready to pledge himself body and soul. Noel didn't deserve him. But he loved him.

He made his mouth shape the words, took a breath and tried again. Opened his eyes, and Izzy was watching with bright-eyed solemnity, trembling slightly.

"It's all right if you can't—"

"Shut up. I love you, Izzy. Truly I do. I didn't think I had to say it for you to believe me."

"I never doubted. But I wanted to hear it. And I wanted it to be you who said it to me."

"Then let me say it again: I love you."

"Thank you."

"Thank you?"

"For caring at all. For being everything."

And then it was simple. Then it was only the joy of kissing Izzy, of making him gasp and arch and splay his legs, Noel finding as much thrill in causing him pleasure as in receiving it from him. He rolled so Izzy was on top of him, as they had been on the floor at home. Except here they were safe, and naked, and in love. Admittedly, completely, with nothing to hide.

"So now what, Mr. Peters?" Izzy purred, Noel's pearling cock sliding between his buttocks.

"So now you're gonna slick up like the tart you are and ride the spunk out of me with that tight little hole of yours."

Izzy shuddered deliciously, humping forward, his prick slapping Noel's belly. "You are a filthy fucker, aren't you?"

"Trained by the best. Now get to it. I want you squirming."

In record time Izzy complied, bringing the jar of petroleum jelly back to the bed and climbing on directly. Every way of having Izzy was delightful, but Noel wanted this. Wanted Izzy atop him, winding his hips as he sought to enclose Noel. Wanted the sound Izzy always made when it happened, a startled murmur like he hadn't believed it possible. Craved the flutter of Izzy's eyelashes and the trembling of his lips, his body perfectly still, poised on that precipice where to move was to end everything.

The crisis passed, and Izzy moved, with four beastly shoves took Noel completely, so sudden it took all of Noel's effort not to spend on the instant. He owed Izzy more, owed him everything. Whatever the fool wanted that to mean.

"I figured it out," he murmured. "It don't matter if you're a man or a woman, if one of us is rich."

"How's that solve—"

"Easy," Noel said with a bump of his hips. "I'll make a fortune. Then I'll straight up hire you. Exclusive like." He wrapped his hand round Izzy's cock then thrust, jolting him hard. "I'm not sharing this." He thrust again, as in love with the delirious expression on Izzy's face as with the feel of his tightness around him. "And every night. I'll come home from wherever I made my fortune, and you'll be waiting for me."

"I'll hear your key in the door and run up to bed," Izzy panted, swivelling round Noel's shaft, ever the tease.

"Strip yourself."

"Grease myself."

"Yes. Get ready for me to come in and throw you down and give it to you just like this."

"Christ almighty...Mr. Peters..."

"Don't you dare spend," he growled, shifting his grip lower on Izzy's cock, his thumb on the pressure point. "Not till I'm done with you."

"Yes, Mr. Peters."

"Fuck, why is that so good to hear you say?" Still gripping Izzy, Noel thrust. Again, then unstoppably, and for all that he'd wanted to last forever, to never ever stop, the clasp of Izzy around him was too much to deny, too good to resist. Before he'd had nearly enough, the crisis was upon him, tearing through his self-control. He let go of Izzy's cock, grabbed his thighs instead, to hold him down, make him take it, every drop of sperm, every yearning inch, all he had to give. His everything.

Incensed

Mr. Everley's visit counted as one of the most unpleasant experiences in Ursula's life. Right up there with giving birth, and discovering her husband was not only deceased but a bigamist. She had survived both those crises through her own competence and determination. This was so far beyond her control she could barely comprehend.

Why hadn't Everley simply arranged another booking for his master? He could have bought out the whole House every night for a year and barely noticed the expense. There was of course no glory in chasing captured prey, like hunting tame fowl on a well-groomed estate. Not for the first time, Ursula pondered the perverse law of attraction that made privileged men seek danger. It seemed that the safer their upbringing, the fiercer their need for something which felt like adventure. Ruining young men: a pastime fit for a prince.

Incensed, Everley had kept saying. Like his master was a

smouldering cinder, which wasn't far from it, a hot body able to burn her world to the ground. The demand was that Izzy present himself to apologize, in whatever way his highness deemed sufficiently debasing. She had not agreed. It made no difference. Not one of her allies had the power to intervene. Given her other problems, she'd been calling in a lot of favours of late. To save Izzy, she'd have to use yet another.

And then the evening was upon them, and the custom began to arrive. Most passed through the receiving room with no more than a blush and a civil nod of the head, her cold reputation a reliable defence against the conversation of men buying sex. Later than expected, the inner door opened and her boys came in, more or less dressed for work, though Izzy's tie was unknotted and he'd not combed his hair. They were however smiling, at least until they saw her expression.

"Don't tell me," Izzy said tightly. "You've had a very nasty visit today from a very angry man."

"His secretary."

"Fucking hell."

Footsteps echoed from the basement stairs, and Ursula got to her feet. She hadn't moved from the chair where she'd sat to receive Everley, and her hips seemed to creak audibly as she stood. "Come, we'll speak in my office."

They followed her to the much smaller chamber behind the receiving room. Here she kept only a writing table and a few chairs, giving preference to a large combination safe bolted to the stone floor. Thieves had found and emptied it more than once, not knowing that the majority of the takings never passed through it. Advance credit, which prevented a gentleman from acting ungentlemanly by welching on his debts, was a wonderful mechanism for keeping her enterprise solvent.

The little stone-walled room was dim, lit by a single kerosene lantern which she brightened before sitting at the writing table. "First, tell me, are you hurt?" she said to Izzy.

He shook his head briefly. Noel sat upright, eyes flashing. "Like hell you ain't. Show her the marks."

"She don't need to see the marks."

"Damn well near choked him."

"I panicked."

"Of course you bleeding panicked—"

"You haven't got to shout about it—"

"Gentlemen..."

Both men checked themselves, sat back in their chairs, fuming. Noel was the first to speak again. "So now what? How are we supposed to manage this?"

"I believe Mr. Pound should leave London as soon as possible."

"I bleeding well knew it," Izzy said. "I knew you were going to say that."

Noel looked back and forth between them with increasing panic. "You mean that's the end of it? One scuffle, and that's it, run for the hills?"

"Of course," Izzy groaned. "A man like him ain't meant to even be looked in the eye by rubbish like you and me."

Noel wiped a hand over his face. "And so if he goes, what about me? What do I do?"

"For now, nothing," Ursula said.

"Nothing?" he gaped.

"Unless you think you ought to go with him."

"No," Izzy said, his jaw set. "God knows where I'll end up. I can't do that to him. Ruin his life too."

"Fucking hell, Pound. You saying...all that before, then running off to wherever? Yeah, a real gift, thank you so bleeding much."

"For fuck's sake, Peters—"

"Save it, I'm late for work." Noel got up abruptly, stalked out of the room without looking back. The click of the door closing struck Izzy hard, and he hunched forward and buried his face in his hands.

Ursula locked the door, then went to the safe, opened it and took out the squarish envelope containing Izzy's gratuities of the prior two years. She came and sat in the chair beside and set her hand on his quaking shoulder.

He turned to her with a haunted look. "He knew my parents' names," he grated. "Where on earth did he find that out?"

"Should we be concerned for their welfare?"

"The pain in the arse is like to have 'em killed just for spite."

"Let's hope he only used the information as a threat."

"Either way, I'm better off leaving sooner rather than later, ain't I?"

"You aren't without resources, however. I've been meaning to address this with you." She handed him the envelope.

"Is this what I think it is? My tips?"

"Not to the penny, but it was what could be easily given you on short notice."

He took the banknotes out and fanned through them. "Cor...you mean this isn't all of it?" he murmured. "Not to say this isn't an awful lot."

"I could give you the exact figure."

"Nah...s'all right. I can count..." He splayed the banknotes again, feeling their texture between thumb and finger.

"I hoped this might improve your outlook."

"This is the best news I could have got, other than RP dropping dead."

"RP?"

His royal pain," Izzy said absently, still handling the notes. Then he looked up. "D'you suppose I ought to get a bank account? It feels risky as, stepping out with this much ready on my person."

"I'll make some inquiries. In the meanwhile we should be able to provide you credit through a solicitor with whom I have dealings."

He chuckled dryly, stuffing the notes back in the envelope. "Banks and solicitors. If I wasn't running for my life to keep from being molested by Prince Muck of Muckingham, you'd think I'd turned respectable. But hang on," he said with a canny look. "If I've got to get out of town, I can't be waiting around for credit from solicitors and such."

"That's another bit of good luck. I have a friend able to provide lodgings, for as long as you need."

He laughed again. "Ain't that convenient. It's almost like you're trying to get rid of me."

"Nothing could be further from the truth, Mr. Pound. I simply take precautions. I hate that this has happened to you."

"You and me both, ma'am."

STAY OR GO

Izzy never showed up in the salon that evening. He wasn't in the room neither, nor the lounge downstairs. Noel did his level best not to think about him, but the absence was hard to ignore. Noel had got used to hearing that broad laugh, to spying that smirk past the pallid faces of the clients. To knowing he wasn't bearing the brunt of the custom's attention.

He stuck near the bar, which is where they were used to finding him. It gave him an out: he was already occupied in aiding Sal, thanks, but perhaps another time. Which tended to make them offer more money. Rose had been right, of the clients he'd had, none had dared to mention his colour, seeming more interested in his maleness, his strength.

Midweek, the salon was sedate. As he leaned back with his elbows on the bar, observing the few couples ensconced in corner couches, Noel realized he hadn't seen Marisol since that dreadful reservation, her disdainful comments another voice missing from the choir. Prue was approaching, and he stepped behind the bar to pour a glass of the raspberry cordial she liked.

"Ah, thanks Noelly. You're a sweetheart."

"Speaking of, what's the goings on with Marisol. I've not seen her in days."

She lowered the glass, licking her lips. "Me neither. I think she's gone home."

"What, St Johns Wood?"

"No, France." She took another sip as the salon door opened. Noel of course looked, and so did Prue, who sighed a little on recognizing the grey-whiskered fellow. "Oh, crumbs. I'm likely needed again." She gulped down the cordial and passed Noel the glass. "Thanks ever so much."

She hurried away, leaving Noel with even more to think about. Mainly that he ought not to have left Izzy's side. Not if Marisol had had to run off all the way to bleeding France. The regret had ground away at Noel since he'd stomped out of Ursula's office. Izzy had only been thinking of his best interests, hadn't wanted to put him at risk. It didn't matter what they said to one another in private. Saying you loved someone didn't protect them. It hadn't changed a thing about their lives, the danger they were in.

He had taken Izzy's departure as a rejection, too new at caring for someone to know how to do it well. Yet it was Izzy who'd said it first, who said it the most, said *I love you* as easy as breathing, as smiling. And Noel had thrown that back in his face, and then stormed off. He'd been the one to leave.

And now the question: to stay or to go? Stay overnight

at the House, hoping Izzy turned up or had perhaps never left, had hidden in Ursula's rooms; or go back to their flat in case Izzy had taken his chances alone? He delayed to the last then practically ran home, arriving in a lather to find the flat empty. Untouched since that afternoon to judge from the cold tea in their cups, Izzy's shirt drying on the back of the chair.

Sleep came hard, the bed frigid without another body, such that Noel slept in his clothes. He woke to the hammer of rain. Pulled the blankets over his head and cried. One night—not even, a scant two hours, and everything was ruined. All their plans, their desires, hopes, loves: nothing when set against the whim of one high-born man. And there was not a thing on earth Noel could do about it, except lay alone in this cold room and feel his loss.

Even these tears were an indulgence, a waste of time, when his duty was to be on his feet and out the door and on his way back to the dirt he ought never to have left. He should have told Pound to get stuffed, that night he'd come swanning in. Should have told him to take his nobby suit and polished shoes and sinful job and all his promises and jump in the stinking river. Instead Noel had let him get inside his heart, carve a hole, then leave it gaping.

Enough. Get up. Get on.

He walked until the omnibus caught up, then rode to as close as it took him to the bridge. The rain had eased, and old Tork had set up his cart in front of the shuttered Lion's Head, doing a brisk trade in Cornish pasties. Though his guts felt like mud, Noel obliged himself to buy one. He stood with the other labourers under the eaves of the pub to eat it. But the food was restoring, the meat well-seasoned, maybe even turmeric in the yellow dough, and it was pleasant to stand in companionable silence with men who wanted nothing from him. Who didn't smell like soft soap and pedigrees but earth and sweat and effort. Him and Izzy weren't cut out for the upper-crust. If he saw—no, shut up, *when* Noel saw him, once they were together again, he'd get them off this luxury treadmill.

By whatever magic of weather, the rain hadn't hit so hard at this end of the city, and the soil was merely wet and not a sluicing mud-pit. Mickey was already at it, bow-backed over the swedes, the cabbages he'd cut earlier stacked under a canvas. He took Noel's praise with a grunt and a nod and kept on. Noel dug into his own tasks, glad of the pasty warming his insides, and of the normalcy, right down to his ma and pa griping at each other across the rows. They even got a bit of sun, lancing through a ragged tear in the clouds and making the raindrops on every surface shine.

Most of the work was done by noon. As Mickey was cleaning the muck off the spades and such with a bucket from the brimming rain cistern, Noel joined his father on the old bench by the riverbank. Someone had rebuilt the bench so it hardly creaked under them, and they sat in quiet, his father now and then clearing his throat and spitting into the grass.

Noel was tired but at ease. If he could have put up his feet, he'd have had a little kip, right here on the bench. But then he'd miss Izzy, if he happened to come home. "I ought to get on."

"Always in a rush now, Noelly."

"I'm a busy man, Pops," he chuckled.

"You'll run yourself ragged, if you no take care."

"I know. I'm not hard done by, though. Nelson's room's turned out to be right comfortable."

"Even sharing with that Pound fellow?"

"Izzy? He's all right. We ain't there much at the same time."

"He a busy man too, eh?"

"It's the way of the modern world, ain't it?"

"So they tell me."

To think of Izzy was naturally to worry. The fool might be scaling the roof right now, and Noel wasn't there to let him in. "I better go."

He would have got up, but his father put his thick hand on Noel's knee, gave him that straight-into-your-soul look that only a father had. "Something gnawing on you, son?"

There was no lying to him. Or he'd send in Noel's mother to extract the truth, with tears and slaps and guilt. "You're a savvy old goat, you know that?"

"Savvy as."

"It's maybe nothing, but...well, I ain't seen Pound in a night and a day. It's unusual."

"He in trouble?"

"Most likely. He had a row, a proper set-to, with some lord or other."

"And now you ain't seen him."

"Yeah."

Whatever advice his pops had, he was taking his merry time giving it. Instead he sat and watched the skiffs scooting up and down the middle channel of the river, too shallow at low tide for heavy boats. If Noel's father couldn't see a way out of this nightmare, what chance did

Izzy have?

"I've got to get on. Sorry, but."

His father waved it away. "No worry. Go on with you. God help your friend."

Crossing the bridge towards the city, Noel dithered between heading to the flat and heading to Ursula's straight off. He hated entering Mayfair in his work—his farm work—apparel. Again the image rose of Izzy clinging to the roof. Home it was.

No Izzy. No dead man lying in the yard, but no living man in the bed, the flat, anywhere around. Noel washed up, changed into his street suit then laid down. Pretended he'd be able to rest. Got up and paced for a few minutes, sat in the chair, stood up again. Grabbed at his hair and pulled until his scalp was shrieking.

Wonderful, now he looked as mental as he felt. Teeth clenched against the shout that was building in his lungs, he jammed his old hat—Izzy had taken his new one—over the stuck-up nap of his hair, made sure the window was unlatched and propped open at least one finger's width, then left for the House.

The rain was done and he was hours early, so he chose to walk, hoping it might burn off the nervous energy rocketing around inside him. Coming into the better borough, he checked his stride, straightened his jacket, making himself seem irrelevant. Some clerk's boy, running from office to office, not worth stopping to question, even if the copper had a quota to fill.

He paused at a corner for a parade of cabs and delivery carts to pass. Beside him stood a squarely-built gent with curling blond sideburns and gloves so clean they shone. He gave Noel a second glance, and then a third.

"House of Lords?" he murmured, now looking ahead so that Noel wasn't fully sure he'd heard him.

"Beg pardon?"

"That's where I've seen you," the toff said more clearly, with a sidelong glance that made Noel shiver.

"I'm afraid I don't know what you mean, sir." So Ursula had told him to answer, feigning complete confusion.

"Perhaps I've mistaken you for someone else." The road cleared and the toff stepped off the curb. Someone bumped Noel from behind and he woke up to his circumstance, standing like a pillock in the middle of Mayfair.

The rest of the journey passed like a dream. Not a sunny daydream but a terrorizing landscape of surreal imagery. He kept catching up to the man with the sideburns and had to lay back and fake an interest in the contents of shop windows, all the while watching the crowd's reflection for other threats. Every coach bigger than a pony-trap was suspect, every white man without a moustache might be Everley. Everyone that passed was a potential grasser. He wasn't safe until he was indoors.

At last Spencer Street. The House inhabited an odd little bit of it, the nearest corner a narrow wedge that meant Ursula's custom exited not through the entry but from the rear of the building by a door onto the mews behind. For how many centuries had men being paying to pass through that stone-walled salon? More years and men than bore thinking of, and with his usual mingling of shame and relief Noel cut behind the billboard that obscured the alleyway to the staff's even more clandestine door. A miniature fortress, hidden in plain sight.

And here was its dragon, the bull mastiff called Nellie, pet to the doorman Clyde who was more or less a bull mastiff in human form. As Nellie smelled him over, Noel stood very still, having never gotten past his childhood memories of being bit by his uncle's pit dog, who'd left a ugly line of scars dotted down his right calf. This leg itched something fierce as Nellie snuffled about his feet. Satisfied, she ambled away toward her hutch by the entranceway.

Ursula wasn't in the receiving room or even her little office, and Noel mooched back down the corridor, regretting his haste in coming. No one was likely to be about for some time, leaving him alone with his sour thoughts, but as he reached the turn he met Annie, coming from the lounge he guessed for she hadn't a coat or hat. "You're in early, Noelly."

Blast, in her Geordie accent his name sounded like the dog's. "Howzit, Annie. Is herself about?"

"Upstairs, I expect. If it's important she'll not mind seeing you. Last door to the left."

It was as always very quiet upstairs, a touch of damp in the air and the stale scent of old carpeting. He tapped on the door, then wondered if she'd heard, and was about to knock again when the chain lock rattled loose and the door opened.

"Good afternoon, Mr. Peters."

"Where is he?" What had happened to his manners, to his, *good afternoon to you, ma'am, sorry to disturb*?

Who gave a damn, for he'd never seen Ursula express such uncontrolled emotion, as her lips thinned and her eyes softened, her unyielding shoulders drooping. "I'm so sorry, Mr. Peters."

She might as well have struck him, for he fell back, clutching his roiling stomach, his heart threatening to tear itself loose and burst straight out of his chest. The lights seemed to swell then dim, and he was suddenly sitting down, slumped against the wall, Ursula crouching beside him.

"Noel, he's alive. I meant that I can't tell you where he's gone."

"Fucking hell, ma'am," he gasped when he could breathe again.

"I intended to speak with you this evening. I'm sorry to surprise you."

"He didn't even say goodbye. Last time we spoke was in your office. When I more or less told him to get stuffed."

"I'm sure he forgives you. And if you aren't feeling well, you needn't feel obliged to work this evening. You seem weary."

Not working meant having nothing to do but think. "Nah, I'll grab a kip and be right as rain. And truth be told I wouldn't mind a chance to beat the ever-loving out of someone."

She lowered that motherly gaze at him. "Don't let your feelings make you careless, Mr. Peters."

"Yes, ma'am."

Bad News

Ursula had hoped that Noel's shock was the worst that would happen that day. Though she had little faith in anything beyond the visible, she had observed a general pattern that if the evening started poorly, it would end well. Bad news was good for business. Most of the time.

When she and Noel got downstairs, he went for a lie down and she went to her offices. Sal the bartender was fidgeting on one of the chairs by the coal brazier in the receiving room, a crumpled letter in hand.

"Good afternoon, Sal."

"Ma'am," they replied tersely. Their voice had lost much of its depth, and their jaw was trembling.

With a sick feeling, Ursula sat in the other chair. "Have you received bad news?"

"That's putting it mildly, ma'am. He found me." Sal thrust the letter at her. *My Dreamy Baby*, it began. On it went in an oppressive, treacly style, calling Sal all manner of childish endearments—baby wife, little girl—and Ursula had read only a little before Sal sprang up from their chair to stalk the room, their teeth bared.

"I'm not going back to Philly," they spat. "I can't go back to living with him. I'll murder the son of a bitch, first time he lays a hand on me. And then they'll send me to the chair. And—"

"Sal, please stop. You're getting carried away."

Sal whirled about, clawing at their cuff to expose the puckered scars up their inner arm. Burned by Sally's husband Stanley, before Sal had shorn off their hair and snuck aboard a British merchant steamer and left that part of their life behind.

"You think I'm joking? That piece of shit so much as breathes on me, I'll tear his throat out with my bare hands." Sal pulled down their sleeve, panting like a runner. "You'd think fleeing the country and quitting womankind and becoming a reprobate and working in a bordello would be enough cause for the piece of shit to divorce me. I mean, how much duress do I gotta put him through?"

"Leave it with me, Mr. Hastings. I'll see who I know that might help."

Sal smiled crookedly. "Geez, ma'am, I don't know what you're gonna be able to do. I don't want to drag you down too."

"Any help I provide will be most discrete, Mr. Hastings."

"Thanks, ma'am."

"Will you be safe this evening?"

"Are you kidding me? Nowhere on earth's as safe as behind your bar."

Blowing into a paisley handkerchief, Sal left the office. Ursula stood up carefully. Her back was plaguing her lately, no matter how closely she tied her corsets, how well she padded them where they pressed against her malformed spine. The basement door opened and Clyde came in, his face unusually pale. The hulking mute was normally unperturbable, but his hand shook as he passed her a small black-edged card. "Thank you, Clyde."

He didn't nod, only glared at the card. No wonder, for he despised the man who'd sent it. The messenger would be waiting below for her reply. She went to her desk and wrote the time at which she was available, then handed the card back to Clyde, who took it with great reluctance before stomping back downstairs.

Of all the men in London, perhaps in the world, there was one whose requests she always fulfilled. Lord Bolton might even be able to assist Sal. Being deputy chief of the metropolitan police force did grant a man certain advantages. One of which was Ursula herself. In truth she needed the catharsis. Whether or not Bolton could provide Sal any assistance, he'd do Ursula a wealth of good.

No more disasters infringed on the afternoon. The staff came in, then the first of the clients. Ten minutes before her own reservation, Ursula locked the back office and made her way upstairs to her personal suite. Clients with abnormal requests would be managed by the staff themselves, or wait until she was free to negotiate. Bless the British propriety that kept the custom well-mannered. She'd done tours of continental bawdies which had stunned her with their lewdness, the unfettered behaviour of the johns.

In due time Lord Bolton arrived. She had stayed dressed, not knowing his full intent, and was sitting by the low-banked fire enjoying the solitude when he entered, locking the door behind him. She was prepared to greet him cordially, but he crossed the room and knelt before her and took her hands in his, then bent and kissed them.

"Romantic fool," she murmured, the quaver in her voice betraying all she felt. When he raised his head she leaned near and kissed him on the mouth. Their first time had been her mistake. An attempt to bribe a handsome senior constable out of arresting one of her girls, back when she'd only had Owen's house by Leicester Square. He'd fucked her gladly, then arrested the runaway. Then come back a week later and paid for it. Three years later, after she'd acquired this House, she'd acquired Harry Bolton's child. The girl was being brought up by Bolton's sister and believed her mother to be deceased, there being no other way to secure her future.

And so Ursula could not refuse him. Did not want to, except that it tore at her heart to have such goodness in such very small doses, twice, three times a year, with no expectation of more. He would not leave his wife, not without losing everything, including Esmerelda. A tangled web, intractable.

He pulled back from their kiss. "I've missed you."

"How is she?"

He chuckled lovingly. "Wonderful. They got her a pony. Thing can clear about a three-inch jump."

"And her teeth?"

"She's lost two since March. Both upper canines at once, the poor rabbit."

Ursula wanted more, to hear every detail, for him to describe her every freckle, every eyelash, every laugh, every joy. They had two hours. "I've missed you as well."

His hands were still wrapped around hers, and he bowed over them again. "Unmake me, my lady."

THE END FOUND THEM together in bed, his head in her lap as she petted his sweat-soaked hair, his heated face. "I have bad news," he murmured.

"Interesting how you waited to share it."

"You would have likely made me leave if I'd told you at the start."

"Is it so bad?"

"If only because it goes so far above my power to amend. My hands are tied, as they say." With a huff of laughter, he raised his hands, the marks left by her ropes clear round each wrist. "I'm afraid this is Foreign Office business. What arrangements have you made for closing down your shops?"

She ceased stroking his hair. "You're right. I would have made you leave." *If not throttled you on the spot.*

He sat up. "Do you wish to hear the entirety?"

"I must. Only, I think I'll have some brandy. And you ought to dress."

He brought her the drink then dressed quickly and returned to the bedside. "Before I tell you anything, I might ask if certain men are clients of yours."

"I can't disclose such information."

"If they aren't, you might get by. If they are...then you're sunk."

She stared at him, chilled by his blank expression. She drank the rest of the brandy in a swallow then thrust the glass at him. He wordlessly obeyed, filling it nearly halfway. Then he settled beside her to tell his tale.

She hardly believed it, but such was privilege, a sort of hypnosis that could lead the powerful to their own ruin. Men—important men, sensible men, men whose names she certainly knew, who ought to have thought harder about their choices—were suspected of passing valuable information to foreign spies working the glamorous side of London's underworld. Courtesans, loan sharks, dealers at high stakes casinos. "Women like your staff," Harry added. "Not streetwalkers, but those who serve the sort of men suspected."

"I trust my staff. Not a one could be involved."

"The onus will unfortunately be on you to prove it. Have you women from other countries working for you?"

The question didn't merit answering, considering her own foreign origins. "England's crawling with newcomers."

"Hence the panic," he said wryly. "Quite frankly, I think it's more to do with placating the morality squad. This is turning out to be a convenient way to close establishments such as yours in a hurry."

"We're not even at war with anyone."

"Yes, but we are in ongoing détente with plenty. The wheels are in motion. I wish it were in my power to change." The higher Harry had climbed in the force, the more influence he had, yet the more eyes were turned upon him. A constable could lose a report, choose not to issue a ticket. The second highest man on the force was under constant scrutiny. How he could not then be a suspect, given his activities...

"This is insanity," she breathed.

"I know." He would have said more but she put up her hand.

"Please leave."

"Ursula, I—"

"Leave, or I am afraid that I will injure your lordship." That she used his stiffest form of address was her sign that their time was at an end. He lowered his eyes, went to put on his jacket.

When he'd gone, she raised her glass, blinking at the fumes, but what was the good in drinking? She drew back her arm to fling the glass at the door as if it was Bolton's head. Would then have to spend hours picking glass out of the carpet.

She drank the brandy.

GRATUITIES

IF IZZY WAS SAFELY away, there was no point in Noel going back to the flat, and he slept at the House that night. He still woke at dawn, though the bedroom was dark as a crypt with only the outline of the door to show him where he was, for the corridor lamps were always lit.

His right arm smarted, sharply in his forearm, more dully in his shoulder. His mood last night had matched the custom's appetites, and he'd done what seemed a school-room's worth of birching of their worthless backsides.

At least he could have a tea while he readied to leave for the gardens. Relying on memory, Noel felt his way to the wardrobe and his thick robe, then slipped into his untied shoes and left the room. Nellie was standing at the bend in the corridor, but the creature had taken him for granted, and went back to her hutch without further fuss while Noel went the other way.

He'd never been around the House at this hour. The

lounge belowstairs was dim, lit feebly by a pair of fluttering gas mantels set in the wall and the coals behind the grate of the enamel stove. He stoked this up and set a kettle to heat, then sat at one of the dressing tables to wait. What an array the women had, all their jars and pots, atomizers of scent, curling rods and papers and pins, paper and silk flowers. They'd stuck pictures around the mirror: cut-outs from magazines and catalogues, postcards of the sea, of famous places. Photographs too, of Annie sitting on Noreen's lap under a photographer's tasselled awning; a goggle-eyed young Prue standing with her stern family; Eloise with a child in her arms. A child who looked just like her.

He was naïve to think it wasn't the case for at least a few of his co-workers. Some were married. He couldn't imagine being on the outside of this, being the one waiting at home. Either he and Izzy were in it together, or not at all. As he was pouring the tea, Ursula came down, leaning hard on her walking stick.

"Good morning, Mr. Peters."

"Ever the professional, I see."

"Consistency is its own reward."

"There's plenty in the pot. You want a cup?"

"Please. No sugar."

"I know."

"Then we might go up to my office. I've something I hoped to give you today."

Carrying both cups, he followed her to her little hidey hole at the back of the receiving room, where she sat on a stool in front of the big safe and began to work the combination. Wishing he'd put trousers on, Noel sat and waited.

Ursula took an envelope from the safe and gave it to him then went to sit at her desk, groaning very softly as she eased herself into the chair. "I thought it only fair as I'd disbursed to Mr. Pound to do the same for you."

"Disbursed? What do you—" He needn't have asked. The answer was here in his hands, in this stack of crisp pound notes, fivers thrust among them. How much? Twenty quid? Thirty? More?

"Your gratuities, Mr Peters."

"But they generally pay me in hand," he stammered. And they did, nightly pressed shillings and farthings on him, just for serving drinks, never mind the standard charges collected for a trip Upstairs.

"Recently some have found you're worth even more," she said. "Shall I reserve it for you a little longer?"

"No," he said, fanning through it, marvelling at the readiness of the wealthy to empty their pockets. No wonder Izzy had been able to skive off so quickly. He'd been at the game for a couple years, worked more in an average week than Noel. "I think I ought hold onto this."

He stayed a little, drinking his tea and making Ursula grin with some of his better stories, but the morning was wearing on and he was needed. His farm gear was at the flat, but he went directly to the garden, following some internal directive that the money had unlocked. Things were moving, the world around him changing, and he was standing still. He was going to get swept away unless he too moved, changed.

It was another sparkling morning, the fog pushed away by a lively breeze that spoke of the colder mornings to come. Reaching his end of the bridge, he sighted down the river to the allotment on the bank, the bobbing dots of colour of his ma and sisters' head-wraps, his father and Mickey two earthy shapes among the green. On the city side of the river, construction scaffold rose above torn-up ground, swarmed over by workmen. They would all be swept away soon. Time to get moving.

His sister Gladys spied him first and stood upright with her hand on her hip. "Nice of you to join us, Sir Hob-badeyhoy. Mind you don't mess your fineries."

"Ease off, will you? I've had a rough couple days. And I can't stay."

"Must be nice."

"Hush, child," their mother said, wiping her hands on her apron. "You in some kind of trouble, my boy?"

"Spare a minute and I'll tell you. You too, Pops. Sorry for leaving you in the lurch."

"Nah, Mickey's been good," his father said. He jammed his spade in the soil, then he and his wife followed Noel to the river.

"You'll likely want to sit down for this," Noel told them.

"Now you've got me scared, Noelly," his mother said as she settled on the bench.

"Sorry, but I've got to be honest with you." *As honest as I can safely be.* A good bit of Ursula's money was in his breast pocket, the rest in the envelope, which he gave to his mother. "Just so you know, I earned every bit of that."

"Lord have mercy…" she murmured, staring at the contents. She looked up, wide eyed. Beside her, his father frowned like a thundercloud as he put his arm around her shoulder.

"You might hate me for this," Noel went on, his voice

cracking. "But I'm going to say it regardless. If I'm not back again, I want you to remember how hard I tried. For all your sakes."

"What you mean, not back again?" his mother said "Why wouldn't you be?"

"I can't say exactly. Only that I've got a feeling."

"We're not taking this," his father said, but when he reached for the envelope his mother clapped her hands shut on it and held it out of his reach.

"Could be something's coming, Pops," Noel said firmly. "I want you all to be ready, in case of anything."

"Rita, you can't take money from your son."

"You take it out of him in labour. What's the difference he wants to give it in ready? Look at our boy. He's in no shortage."

"She's right, Pops, I've got a pocketful."

"See, Lucius? Grant him some common sense. He's your boy, after all. If he's a fool, it's your own fault." She stuffed the envelope in her bodice as her husband sputtered. Then she got up and pulled Noel into a clinging embrace, her bright kerchief barely reaching his chin. "Still my little Noelly, you're always going be."

"Saints above, woman, you'll be the one who turned him fool," his father grumbled, getting slowly to his feet.

"Hush up and thank your son, Lucius."

"Woman—"

"It's not a bother, Ma. It's nothing," he soothed, wishing that applied to all his woes.

He left shortly after, ignoring his sisters' jeers and finding it hard to meet his father's eye. It was for their parents to decide how to spend that money. If it was on paying his replacement in the garden, so be it, the hot flush of guilt not enough to displace his sense of lightness at having perhaps hoed his last ever row of potatoes. Head spinning with potentials, he was almost at the flat before his nerves caught up. None of his dreamy visions of the future came to pass if he was nabbed by Everley and shoved into the RPA's carriage.

He halted at the corner, stepping close to the building to be out of the way of passers-by. Casual like, he leaned on the wall, rolled on his shoulder until he could see round the corner. Rolled back, casual like, then stepped off the wall and began walking calmly away from the pair of con-stables standing at his front door, speaking intently to his landlady.

So that was it for returning to the flat ever again. He'd played this hand well, done his duty to his family and broke their hearts in one. Dodged the coppers. If he got back to Ursula unscathed, it'd be a trifecta. *Except horses don't play cards, you berk*. He heard it in Izzy's voice. With something that was either a laugh or a sob, Noel picked up his pace.

MULDOON

Ursula had drunk far too much of that brandy last night, in the end having to ring the service bell for someone to assist her. She'd woken woolly-mouthed and sour of stomach, feeling like she'd been trampled by cavalry. After the unexpected meeting with Noel, she'd crawled on literal hands and knees up to her room and back to bed for three more hours. When she woke again, her nausea had subsided, replaced by a full-bodied aching, as if a giant hand was squeezing her malformed spine.

Anne was glad to help her mistress with the inversion board in the Hanging Suite. The leather cuffs snug around her ankles, the foot of the board at maximum elevation, Ursula let her arms dangle until her fingers nearly grazed the floor. She so rarely drank and hadn't passed her limits in years, and she deserved every bit of this discomfort. Given what she'd learned from Harry, she needed a clear head. She wouldn't wait to be rumbled, would act in advance, protect her staff and herself before the worst came to pass.

The door opened. "Ma'am, there's someone to see you," Sophie called. "Someone I can't turn away."

"Of course there is," she groaned. "Who is it?"

"Mr. Muldoon. And he's waiting."

Anne leapt up and grabbed the table's handle. "Come and help, you ninny."

In five minutes Ursula was upright and dressed and on her way downstairs. Of all the individuals with which she might be cursed at this moment. A relentless organizer, in the last half decade Muldoon had taken charge of every criminal syndicate between Canary Wharf and Kensington, from the marketplace pick-pockets to the top casinos operating in the back rooms of certain clubs.

He was waiting in the receiving room, finely dressed in grey, legs crossed, a tea cup on his knee. Ursula would praise Sophie for remembering to offer. In person he was better looking than one remembered, with a lean face and expressive eyes. A charming if unremarkable gentleman, until one listened to his words. He did not stand to greet her as she took the chair across.

"Mr. Muldoon. A pleasure to see you."

"Don't lie. It's never a pleasure to see me." If Izzy grew up hard and cruel, he'd have such a voice, bluntly obvious in its low origins, edged with a razor's sharpness.

"I'd rather err on the side of politeness."

"A wise decision. I won't mince words, my dear. It's been made known to me that you are facing a wealth of intractable problems. Which puts you in a state of some desperation. This is of course my ideal scenario. Not because I like to see you suffer," and at this he paused to smile appallingly. "But because it advantages me financially."

"In what way, may I ask?"

"You may. The fact is, my dear, whatever whispering's been going on between lords and whores is but a drop in the bucket of your woes. Or has the Admiral not been to see you yet?"

She blinked. Exhaled very slowly. She might as well be sitting naked before Muldoon, if he knew about the Admiral. "No. He has not."

"Pity. Or not, if you're the sort who likes to ruin people's lives." He smiled again, set his tea aside. "Long story short, he's been to see me. And he made me a most interesting offer. One I find it impossible to resist."

"An offer?"

"Thanks to some very gullible lords, not a man in Whitehall presently wants to be associated with your trade. Our trade, for as you know I've got most of it in hand. Your Admiral wants out in a dreadful hurry. And being the generous soul that I am, I've decided to assist him."

She swore very quietly in Norwegian. He chuckled. "Not a clue what that means, but I'm sure it's something along the lines of *I'm completely buggered*. Because although it hurts me terribly to say, you are."

By the explanation which followed the deal was as good as done. Her last, her grandest, her quietest backer, the only one to whom she still owed a penny, would let Muldoon have it all: the business, the building, and all the assets inside. Including the staff.

"They're not mine to include," she said sharply, owing him no further politeness. "My staff are independent operators."

"A quaint notion, I've always thought, but bad for the bottom line. Course, I'll keep them on as they are. Gents pay quite a lot to get their hides tanned by your harlots."

"I have no control over my staff."

"Like I give a damn. Ways and means, my dear. Ways and means."

"Go to hell."

"Been, got sent back." He smiled, the kind of clever smile a man worked on in mirrors so he could put the wind up his enemies. She wanted to kick it in.

"Do you have anything else worth saying?"

He winced as if he'd witnessed someone get injured. "Such hostility. Unbecoming, my dear, when I'm the very person on whose favour your future lies. You and I could settle on some attractive terms between the two of us. I'd keep a woman like you very well."

"I am not to be kept."

"That is a pity, my dear. Because I don't know how else you're going to survive this. Thanks for the cup of rosie. I'll show myself out."

His half-drunk tea sat on the low table before her. The receiving room was made of stone. This time, she threw the cup. At once, Clyde was up the stairs, looking about fiercely for her assailant. He came to her, went down on one knee, broad face paling as he took her hand.

"Please lock the front door."

He nodded, went to comply. When he came back, she hadn't moved, and he knelt beside her again. How was she going to protect him? Under Muldoon's thumb, he became a stooge, a brute, his intelligence denied by the accident which had stolen his voice.

"Help me, please. I've left my cane."

He nodded curtly again, rose and offered both his hands. Standing, she barely came to his shoulder, and with a desperate gasp she put her arms around him and gave into her grief. He held her, his arms like a wall against the world, their affection that of siblings, a family chosen, indivisible. She would not let Muldoon destroy this gentle soul.

After sweeping up the broken crockery, Clyde locked the door from the basement and set Nellie loose in the receiving room. Then he aided Ursula to an armchair in the salon and rang the house bell to summon the rest of the staff. Not everyone was in yet, and she dispersed some general tasks while they waited for three o'clock. If the staff noticed her mood, they left it unmentioned, but Ursula had a great deal of practice in concealing her pain, both emotional and physical.

Muldoon was a beast, but he'd been right on one account. By being so generous with her staff, permitting them to keep so much of their earnings, she'd left herself vulnerable, indebted, reliant on a man's favour. How foolish of her to preference individual freedom over achieving a broader liberty. It was hence her duty to set right if possible.

The time came when all were gathered, seated or standing about the salon in various demeanours, dressed for the street or for work, Brigid with her hair in curlers, Noel behind the bar to keep his nervous hands busy, Sal stoic beside him, the absences of Marisol and Izzy achingly obvious.

"Company, I cannot believe it has come to this, but we may be at an end of our endeavours." The news was, predictably, catastrophic. All was tears and terror, many of the women unable to afford to lose income to a pimp, who would pocket the main, leave them a pittance, beat them if they complained. All forgave Ursula for having remained in the Admiral's debt, for she had given them a taste of a life beyond any they'd hoped when they'd chosen to join the trade.

She accepted their support with grace, allowing their good feelings to convince her even if only for a moment that there was a solution, a way forward. Many pledged all their ready earnings to the cause, in case the Admiral might be swayed to sell his stake to Ursula directly. It was nothing like enough. Her own funds were far from liquid, could take weeks to liberate. Every solution was its own obstacle.

By now it was nearly five in the afternoon. Custom would be passing, irate that their keys weren't admitting them. There was no good to be had in not working. Money was power, and they needed every bit of it. She got Clyde to help her back to the receiving room, where he settled her on the sofa, stoked the coal brazier to warm her, brought her the mail which she'd failed in the ruin of her day to open, then went to unlock the doors.

LESLIE

The terrible feeling coming all over Noel was not a bit relieved by Ursula's bleak expression as he joined her in the receiving room.

"Please sit, Mr. Peters," she said dully.

"Fucking hell."

"Yes."

Noel shivered, his foreboding sharpened into fear, for normally Ursula scolded him for swearing, or at least gave him a sharp look. Instead she sat bowed, a letter in her shaking hand. He sat across from her. Waited.

"I'm afraid I have made yet another grave miscalculation, Mr. Peters."

"We'll get it sorted, ma'am."

"This is to do with our Mr. Pound."

Again that strike to the gut. Good that she'd told him to sit. "What's happened to him?"

"Although I am unable to confirm his whereabouts or wellness, our Mr. Pound may be facing some unforeseen difficulties.

"Plain English, ma'am."

"The safe haven to which I have sent him is no longer safe." She waved the letter vaguely. "My associate informs me that her own establishment has been summarily closed. And demolished."

"Demolished?"

"A mob, at first. Took it on themselves to stage a raid. Started a fire. The city let it burn out."

"Shit. Ma'am…"

"He couldn't have been there. Might still be on route."

"But he'll have nowhere to go."

"He has lodgings. He won't have to sleep rough."

"Stop. Stop telling me." Noel grabbed at his hair again, wanting to scream, vomit, stand up from his chair so he could smash it to bits. Why shouldn't this happen? He'd dared to wonder what was left to happen, and God had summarily answered. Without waiting to be dismissed, he rose and went back to his room. He wasn't safe outside. Miraculously, by six o'clock he was bored of being terrified, and he finished dressing, went to the salon in search of idle chatter, pretty women, a man to absorb some pain. Rose was by the bar and he joined her, staying on the public side.

"What a cock-up, eh Noelly?"

"Ain't it just. Wish like hell I'd gone with Izzy, to be honest. Milky bastard didn't even tell me he was going. Not that sudden like."

"And so far, too." She shivered, rubbing her hands. "Liverpool's dreadful this time of year."

"How do you—reckon he'll manage?" He had nearly

asked how she knew at all, but it was far more important to find out what details he could.

"Mrs. Gummage at the rooming house is a good soul. She's an old moll herself. Mad as mist, but a real dear."

"Is her house near that bawdy?"

"Why? You aren't thinking of running off too?"

"Ursula said the shop's been knocked down," he said with a stab of guilt for telling what his employer had not.

Rose's face fell. "So then what's Izzy doing?"

He shrugged, the guilty heat in his guts turning to liquid terror as she gazed at him, such pity in her eyes he had to look away. "Renfield Lane," she murmured. "I ought not to tell you, but. The rooming house is called The Manse. You'll know if you see it."

"Perhaps I just want to write him a letter," Noel said, trying, failing to keep the quaver from his voice.

Rose gripped his arm, leaned near and whispered. "For the love of God, be careful. I want you back in one piece."

"That makes two of us. And thanks." Down the far end, the salon door opened, and Sir Sideburns himself walked in. Noel turned to the bar. "Sal, give us a lift, will you?"

"Can do." They poured him a measure of anisette, which Noel had once disliked but lately found himself craving. He drank it back, then faced the room as Sir Sideburns approached him.

"I knew it," the man said. "When I saw you yesterday."

"What was I to say, sir? Hardly fair to expose you like that."

"That was my mistake. Do allow me to apologize."

"Apology accepted."

Leaning on the bar, the man pursed his soft lips. "Really,

you must let me make amends."

"That's not necessary, sir. You meant no harm."

"Heavens, you don't take a hint, do you?" He stroked a finger over the back of Noel's hand. A touch which seemed to burn, and Noel pulled away.

"Sir..."

"I'll pay double."

"I—can't." Lost for how to word the bodily sense of horror rising from the pit of his stomach, he looked desperately to Rose.

"Take pity, Leslie," she said to the man. "Poor chap's just had his heart broke."

"By the saints, Rose! Why'd you tell him that?"

"Oh yes, of course you have," the fellow said gently. "Such a pity. You know, I never thought him such a scoundrel to up and vanish."

"It's not like that," he blurted. "Not at all. He only left town for a while. He'll be back." He hoped.

Rose was speaking with his lordship. Leslie, she'd called him, whose expression was serious as he took his card case from his pocket. He pencilled something on the back of a card then, blushing behind his fair sideburns, turned to Noel.

"Once again, my apologies for speaking rashly. I assure you, I wish only the best for you and your friend. Please, I should like you to take this." He offered the card, which Noel took numbly and shoved in his breast pocket without inspecting. "I await your convenience, my dear," he said to Rose with a bow of his head. He then quit the salon with the mincing step of a man at full mast.

"Never mind, Noelly," Rose said, patting his shoulder.

"You take yourself home. A night off will do you good."
With a last squeeze of his arm, she departed after Leslie,
leaving Noel with his sorrow.

NORTHWARDS

From the horrible meeting in Ursula's office, Izzy had gone straight upstairs to Ursula's own chambers and locked himself in. Managed to keep from going mad thanks to her collection of illustrated marriage manuals and the wealth of new ideas they had generated for his future custom. Not a one of his gents could bend that way. Not without being tied.

The curtains were drawn and he cautiously lifted an edge, not knowing who might have a view, who might be looking to see who was looking. Why was he even still in London? The prick knew exactly where he was, if not here then the bed-sit, which suggested it also was being surveilled. Noel...

Izzy was at Ursula's door before he knew it, ready to unlock it, run downstairs and crab their plans before they'd even got started. None of this was permanent. He had to trust her. Noel was savvy. He wasn't the target. Just the ransom if things got dire. But how hard up could the royal prick be for willing bodies? How many laws of his own nation did he need to break to wet his beak?

Beset with these unpleasantries, Izzy was in a lather when Ursula arrived. She talked him out of most of his fears, and they slept like siblings, comforted by the other's presence in the bed. Much earlier than he liked to be up and about, he was creeping through the foggy dawn to catch the first train bound for Liverpool.

He'd got no further than Birmingham before the bullshit started, as a carefully dressed fellow entered his otherwise empty compartment, set his hat neatly above the seat opposite and sat down. "Hail, fellow well met."

"Morning," Izzy replied, then resumed staring out the window.

The man coughed minutely. "I don't suppose a friend could tease a cigarette out of one."

"Afraid I don't smoke." *And since when am I your friend?* he very much wished to add, but he was in no mood to cause a ruckus.

"Up from London, are we?"

"Nothing gets past you, does it?"

The man smiled broadly, his grey teeth betraying his low origins. "Indeed, nothing does. You had that air about you. That sophistication."

Izzy snorted, made into a sneeze. What in blazes did this fool want? "I assure you, it's nothing of the sort."

"Modesty is such an appealing quality in a man."

Like hell. Not for any money. Even if the prick were selling himself and took Izzy for a likely client. He snorted again. Sat back as the man extended a lavender handkerchief. "That's quite all right. I've got my own."

"There's no pleasing you, is there?"

"Look, I dunno what you're attempting, but if you don't mind, I'd prefer to keep my own company for the duration."

"Where are you bound?"

Fuck me blind, why is this happening? "Northwards."

"What a coincidence. So am I."

"Excuse me, but I might take a walk. The compartment's feeling awful cramped." He stood, grabbing the rack as the train jolted. He snatched his hat and stumbled to the door and out into the corridor and along, ending up in the public lounge car. Good enough, and he found a seat along the wooden banquette and a newspaper to hide behind.

Who had that man been? A ponce, a spy, or just an overly sociable twit? Everyone was an enemy in waiting. He began to feel conspicuous, so made his way back, hoping for, failing to come across a free seat in another compartment.

The prick had pulled down the blinds on theirs, and Izzy stood at the door, debating. He'd paid for the bleeding seat. Second class and all, rather than the open benches of the third. He ought to have splashed out on a reserved seat in First. Then he'd be at risk of running into clients. Of having word passed back to London of where he'd gone.

He rapped on the glass of the door. The corner of the blind lifted and the man peered out. The blind dropped, and the fellow opened the door.

"The prodigal son returns," he murmured as Izzy sat down.

"Pocket it, will you? I've had it up to here with manners and clever talk. From you and everyone. So either keep your thoughts to yourself or I'll be calling the porter and having you tossed for pandering."

"Oh my."

"Don't tempt me." He crossed his arms, went back to staring out the window. The insides of his cheeks were already ragged from being bitten, so he resorted to discretely pinching himself along his side to quell his emotions. He'd not been gone half a day and he regretted it. Rocking with the train, Izzy dug in with his fingernails and prayed for Noel's safety. *Let the danger come after me. Let it pass over him. God, if You're there and You care at all, preserve him.*

The stranger kept quiet and left the compartment shortly after. Other passengers came and went, and Izzy wished he'd brought the newspaper from the lounge. Not to read but as cover. As the day wore on, the hills grew higher, colder, wreaths of fog round their tops, the scale of the landscape hard to gauge. Sitting at a station over a high cutting, Izzy realized with a chill that the grey flecks dotting the wintery turf weren't sheep but houses, tiny at this immense distance. Born and bred in the heart of London, he'd never been farther from the city than Highgate. He might as well be headed to the moon.

On and on, and no good in doing otherwise, for at least he had a destination, wasn't casting himself into the great unknown. He was going to do what he did best, just for someone else for a little. RPA had to have other lads to hassle who might not take his rudeness so personally. There had to be some who liked it.

He had dozed off by the time they reached Liverpool. He had no baggage to retrieve and was soon standing on the pavement before Lime Street station, blinking in the grey afternoon. The northern cold was astonishing, plumes of breath rising from every passer-by. A wind came sweeping up the hill, slicing through Izzy's clothes like they were gossamer.

"A tad underdressed, are we?" The same prick from the train, sauntering down the station steps, buttoning his boiled wool overcoat. Teeth clenched, nothing to say, Izzy stalked off, to hunt for a clothes jobber. What a blessing to have ready money. Or not a bit of this venture was going to be possible.

Swaddled in the same dark stuff as the locals, right down to the felted scarf and lined gloves, Izzy embarked once more. Ursula had given him clear directions and he kept on, towards the docklands. Not exactly to his standards, then. Or at least his newer standards. If he'd gone into the trade for Mrs Owen and not Ursula, he'd have had it harder. Done it harder, probably taken more than given. Funny, he was now a snob about his knob.

These were his sort of people, bowed and grimed and rightfully suspicious of him in his brand new coat and shiny shoes. He ought to have found a rag and bone, got an old coat, avoided being the flash newcomer. What was that about pride going before the fall?

His comeuppance wasn't long in coming, for where the bawdy ought to be was nothing but a yard of trampled mud and burnt timbers and the smell of wet ashes. The brick walls to either side were blackened but largely unharmed. As he gaped at the ruin, another man strolled up, hands in his pockets, collar up. The creep from the train.

He grinned when he saw Izzy, his face falling when he saw the ruin. "Shit. I needed that job."

"Not turn enough tricks on board?"

He laughed harshly. "Not nearly. I've got expenses, lad."

"Expenses...don't come the Rothschild with me. You would have done me for a farthing."

"And you'd have had a marvellous time." He looked at the messy lot again, shaking his head. "Ah well, let's be getting on."

He started walking away. Izzy stared after him. "What d'you mean?"

"Can't be seen standing here. Come along. I'll even buy the first round."

THOUGH LIVERPOOL WAS HARDLY a second comer to London, Izzy had expected merely a brasher, uglier version of the capitol. This was another city entire. Brasher and uglier, yes, but happier and faster of pace, whether from the cold or the industriousness or the pushing enthusiasm of its thousands of immigrants. Izzy crossed streets without hearing a word of Queen's English spoke, red Chinese letters painted proudly on the shop fronts over glistening roast fowl and the heads of pigs in glaze. Everyone else seemed to be Irish.

Without Fawcett dragging him along he might have been sunk, dazzled out of his wits. London was manners and taking oneself too seriously, even amongst its lowest. Fists and fury seemed to get most of the work done around here. Packed shoulder to shoulder at the rail of the fifth, or perhaps sixth public house they'd visited, Izzy's ears rang with the clamour, the snatches of song and the rise and fall of arguments. He was very drunk, more than he liked, but there was beer in his glass and he drank it.

At least he was warm. Truth, he was steaming, like every other man in the place. His companion Fawcett's face was glowing, his mangy teeth and Brummy accent fully exposed as he leaned against Izzy. "Like I said, it's not as if there's no work," he slurred. "A crop of bad luck, but we'll not starve. We'll make our nethers. This place won't do, though."

"Do for what?"

"Wrong crowd. Not nearly desperate enough."

They both ducked at the sound of breaking glass. "Not desperate, you say?"

"The wrong sort of desperation. Bottoms up and we'll away."

"I've had enough." Izzy put down his glass, the murky beer swirling like the river they drew the water from to brew it. With much shoving and glaring, they got out to the street. Fawcett lead them onward, down ever worsening alleys to a much worse pub, if only for the fact that a man was pissing against the front wall within splashing distance of the door. They stopped some ways back on the other side of the street.

"What's the point of coming here?" Izzy muttered.

"Dear me, you are thick," Fawcett replied just as quietly

"I'm out of my element, is all. I'm established back home."

"Isn't that nice? And yet here you are."

The drunk had finished his business and went staggering past but Fawcett ignored him, watching the door of the pub. Izzy began to shiver as the wind sneaked past his clothes, freezing the sweat to his skin. The sun had set hours ago and he thought to check the time, but that meant unbuttoning his coat, letting Fawcett see his watch. He was about to ask what they were waiting for when a brick-shaped man in a pea coat and knitted cap came out of the pub.

The fellow looked about, lighted on them. Jerked his head. Fawcett nodded back. "Won't be long," he murmured to Izzy, then he crossed the street and disappeared into the inky shadow of the lane beside the pub, following the man in the pea coat.

No.

Not for a shilling, a bob, a ten pound note. There was need and then there was pride, and Izzy wasn't nearly so desperate. He had ready in pocket, and the promise of a room, a locked door between him and everything that was trying to undo him. To hell with this Fawcett, breathing down his neck, stroking sailors in the shadows. Izzy was better off alone.

Mrs. Gummage

Of course he got lost, so sloshed that more than once he caught himself looking overhead for Big Ben or St Paul's. He kept finding only the black and boundless river, though that might have been as it was downhill from everything else. Up he went once more, his body sore from shivering, his feet from striking the pavement again and again.

He stuck where there were people, finding comfort in crowds, in the odd lilt of the local dialect. He played with it under his breath, the sounds less clipped than his own, more throaty than a toff's. Given that he could pull off that headmaster's routine for the clients, there was no reason he couldn't pass here as being from somewhere that wasn't London.

A few souls straggled around a chestnut seller on the corner ahead, and he asked them for directions to Renfield Lane, which turned out to be back the way he'd come. Citing his extreme drunkenness and their own, he got them to explain it three times, their Merseyside accents not aided by their collective lack of teeth.

As Ursula had said, one knew the Manse to see it, if only by its bulk, for there had stopped being lamps two streets back. The details could wait, and God help him if the lady of the house didn't answer the door, more than likely at this unlikely hour. He had never been this cold. If she didn't let him in, he'd have to sleep in the bleeding shrubbery and they'd find him frozen to death—

Footsteps. The rattle of locks, the gold flare of a lamp through the bubbled glass transom. The door cracked open and a rheumy eye appeared.

"Ur-Ur-Ursula. Ursula said you had r-r-r—"

"Up from the House, are we?"

He turned his shivering into a nod. The eye retreated, the door swung open, and he came into the warmth. The name Mrs. Gummage had put him in mind of a stolid, lumpy woman, but the lady was a frail thing, translucent of skin, with great moony eyes that didn't blink quite enough. She was wearing a boldly patterned Turkish robe over a number of night dresses, glittering strands of beads round her puckered neck. All of it made stranger by her being tiny, barely reaching his shoulder, and he was hardly a giant.

She blinked up at him, delicate hands clasped under her chin. "Train's been here hours," she chirped. "Or did you come in on the late one?"

"I g-g-g-got caught up with someone."

She nodded, the beads tinkling. "That'll happen." She lapsed into staring at him, and he was just about to remind her why he was there when she clapped her hands, then started for the back of the house. "I suppose you'll be wanting tea. Lucky I'm not much for sleeping these days."

"No tea. Thanks. Just sleep. A room. Please."

"Oh aye. Come up then. I've got but the one." She hoisted the front of her skirts, baring her stick-thin legs half to the knee, then started laboriously up the worn stairs. He followed, wishing he could pick her up and carry her, anything to shrink the time between this moment and sleep.

"You're lucky indeed," Mrs. Gummage said. She let go the rail to adjust her grip on her skirts, swaying on the step so that Izzy put up his hands to catch her. But she grabbed the bannister and kept on. "This room's just come open, it has."

"Someone move out?"

"Moved off, as in this plane of existence." She trilled a little laugh, beads clinking. "But don't mind me, I'm a bleak old bat. He was a right shit, had it coming. You, on the other hand," and she levelled a long finger at him. "You look like a nice young lad. Been at Ursula's long?"

"Two years, thereabouts."

She laughed again, throwing back her head, which seemed too heavy for her lanky neck. "Oh, you've seen nothing, my lad. Two years!"

Still tutting, she resumed climbing, then lead him along a dim corridor. She stopped at a slim door, fished an immense key ring from her sagging pocket and began flipping through the dozens of keys.

"There's a water closet three to your left. Don't disturb the other boarders. I put out mutton at three in the PM but it's usually gone in a flash so it's on you to be on time."

"Duly noted, ma'am."

She hummed, a high derisive sound. "Well, aren't we the formal one? You'll get over that, I don't doubt. Now then, this ought to be it."

She finagled the key off the ring while Izzy swayed, perilously close to falling asleep on his feet. With a grunt she yanked it free, then unlocked and opened the door. It struck something solid which prevented it from fully opening.

He peered in to what appeared to be a largish closet. Never mind swinging a cat, there was hardly room for a man to stand beside the bed, the foot of which was what kept the door from opening.

"I know it's not much," Mrs. Gummage said proudly. "But I don't expect you've a choice at the present."

"It's grand."

"You can pay in the morning. Mind you better, though."

"Yes, ma'am."

She snorted, pulled the key from the lock. "Ursula indeed." She shoved the key into his limp hand, steered him into the room and shut the door behind. He turned, locked the door, shuffled back a step, sat on the bed, laid down, gave up.

It was less like waking and more like unconsciousness had spat him out, for he was suddenly there in his body, aware and thoroughly appalled by the fact. Everything hurt. Inside and out. Except what mattered most.

Groaning miserably with every movement, Izzy rolled onto his back and felt the front of him. His trousers were intact, and some careful probing convinced him he'd not been molested. Halle-fucking-lujah, for he remembered almost nothing of the prior evening, including how he'd gotten to the rooming house, in a bed of which he presumably lay. Much of the pain in his arms was from having slept in all of his clothes. He hadn't even taken off his new coat, which to judge from the smell was a long ways past new.

He lay for a little, eyes closed, teeth clenched. The cistern was three doors to the left. That much he remembered her saying. He shoved the coat off his uppermost arm, wanting the minimum of garments between him and whatever might come out of him. Very bad things were happening to his guts, and he needed them not to happen in bed. He shoved his leaden feet off the mattress and let the swing of his legs pull him upright, all the way to standing.

Straight into the wall, twelve inches away.

"Sweet merciful fuck!" He fell back, clutching his nose, every other pain blanked by the bursting agony, like he'd taken a fist to the face.

"Keep it down, ya doss cunt!" his neighbour hollered in immediate reply, pounding on the wall between. "Some aye us is still sleeping."

He managed. To stand, to properly doff his heavy coat, to reach the WC before any part of him gave way. Gutted, clinging to the poorly painted wall, he retreated to his room. Realized that what he'd taken for a miserably hard pillow was sheets and a blanket, folded. He stared at the stack a moment, then shoved it closer to the head of the bed, put his coat on and laid down and gave up again.

This went on for a while: the waking, the shaking, the staggering three doors to the left and being glad of having done so every time. Gummage came up around noon with a weak tea, a lovely gesture which he poured down the cistern as soon as she'd gone, as it resembled the muddy beer from last night. Was this agony only on account of not being a local? God help him if he wasn't purged of London by the end.

Hollowed out and bored to tears, he forced himself downstairs mid-afternoon. Staked a place in the coffered dining room though the mutton wouldn't be out for some time. It was dim and quiet and warm and safe, though odds were Fawcett was staying here too.

Ah well, the shit could take the cut infernal, learn the sharp end of London snobbery, and for a while Izzy day-dreamed on how he'd do it. Speak over him. Ask Gummage if she'd not taken out the rubbish bins, for he'd caught a whiff of something awful. Or would that spoil his already limited chances in this city?

Fawcett never appeared. Others did, sour of face and odour, ragged of cuff and collar. Izzy shunted down in his chair, crossed his arms and slipped his watchchain into his pocket. No good came of lording it over his fellows. Being new, he was ignored. He took the smallest slice of mutton, compelled himself to eat it. Waited for his guts to still. Finished dressing and went out.

To nowhere. To anywhere. With many a backward glance to fix the streets in his memory, Izzy meandered wherever his feet took him. Ursula had promised to send word to Gummage when her agent up here was able to see him. He was well provisioned, had nearly twenty quid on his person. Enough to last him ages if cautious.

When it was nearly dark, he bought a packet of roast nuts and went back to the Manse. Built of smooth grey stone and tawny plaster, rising two stories and stretching off to each hand, it would have been a grand house in its day but was now stained by decades of soot and its owners' declining fortunes. The front door was left unlocked until eight, and he slipped in and upstairs without encountering anyone.

There wasn't a lamp in his room, so he stood on the landing and slowly ate a few chestnuts. When he went in, the bed had been made up and a candle stub set beside it. So Gummage had her own key. Took liberties. Another friendly gesture, but it meant Izzy had not one safe place, not one door he could close that another person couldn't open. Hearing voices below, he went in to what passed for his room, locked the door as if it made a difference.

LONDON

WAKING THE NEXT DAY was a new form of agony, the return to daily awareness heart-breaking. The dim room had the feel of a monk's cloister or a cell in an asylum, and he dressed and went out straight away. If he could, he'd find a way to earn his bread. The city had yet to defeat him.

Many weary hours later, he was prepared to call it a draw, at least for this round. He'd been to a dozen employment agents, none of whom gave him more than a cursory glance, the postings on their board far beyond his skills. As for the low tasks, there were so many newcomers prepared to take any job there was that one had merely to say the word 'dig' and five men appeared with their own spades, vowing to out-shovel each other. Izzy had savvy, and charm, and acquiescence on command, and no easy way of exploiting these. Getting into house service meant mixing with the upper crust, meant some grotty lord who'd known him down south chasing him round the parlour. Perhaps if he grew out his moustache, they'd not recognize him.

As the evening came on he stopped for a pub meal of a thick brown stew and an ale to match, which he drank in the name of inuring himself to the local poisons. The only free seat left him with his back to the door, and he ate quickly with one eye over his shoulder. For all he knew this was one of the boozers he'd visited with Fawcett.

What a rotten way to live, on the edge of a knife, ready at any moment to bolt, to hide, to dissemble and lie. He ought to have gone to ground at Ursula's for a week or so, stuck it out until the royal pain found another toy. Instead he'd panicked, given up his only safety, his best friend and love, in exchange for this bitter isolation. Hadn't had the cods to say goodbye even. He'd taken all those fine feelings, every word he'd begged Noel to say, and burnt them to ashes, not an hour after.

Deserving this pain didn't make it any easier to bear. Only made it gouge harder, like a hook twisting in his heart, to know that his loss was of his own creation. His guts griping at being obliged to so rapidly expand, Izzy left the public house and wandered on, not minding where he was going. He'd not seen this street before, nor the one it crossed, but there were plenty of folk about, men of all nations, women and children, most heading in the same direction, and he went along, relieved to see he was not the best dressed among them.

In the square ahead was a holiday market, vendors and their carts and stands around the perimeter, and in the centre a grand bonfire, tended by a few men with leather aprons and the forge-bronzed faces of blacksmiths. Warmth, light, cheer, and Izzy drifted here and there, drawing comfort from the carollers, the steaming vats of wassail and the cries of the sellers, the piercing scent of the evergreen boughs used as bunting and strewn underfoot.

In time the lack of a familiar face began to wear. At such an affair at home, he'd have bought one of Betsy's sugar plums. He'd be taking his mum to Advent services. He'd be thinking of a gift for Noel. Something useful, for he'd scorn anything too flash. A new hat perhaps, for the one Izzy had lost.

Standing amongst the crowd by the fire, warmed inside by the meal, by the fantasy of Christmas with Noel, he very nearly didn't notice the soft hand stroke down his side in search of his pocket. Never a moment's rest, and he snatched for, grabbed a slim wrist. It was attached to a scrap of a lad, barely more than a child. Izzy let go and the would-be thief went tumbling back, landing on his arse.

"Whaddya do that for?" the lad cried.

"It's your hand what was in my pocket," Izzy retorted, but the boy scrambled up and darted away through the crowd, who lost interest once it was clear no fight was brewing. If ever there was a sign for Izzy to call it a day. He circuited the marketplace until he reached a street that led in the right direction. He'd had enough novelty, enough disappointment, enough of jumping at shadows and searching the faces of every man for recognition.

"There he is!"

He glanced around, curious that he should have had that thought and then heard it said. The pickpocket was marching towards him up the sloping street, leading a pair of much larger and angrier fellows.

"That's the tosser what knocked me down!" the lad

cried, pointing most definitely at Izzy.

"After I caught him fingering my pockets," Izzy retorted, backing away. "Or was I meant to let him fan me?"

"No one lays a hand on one of our boys," said the one.

"A man's entitled to protect himself."

"You better hope you've some skill in that, London," the other big one said, rocky fists clenched and rising.

The boxing club aside, Izzy didn't stand a real chance against that much manpower. Running for his life it was, again. Yet he'd not gone three strides before one of them grabbed hold of his thick sleeve and yanked him back. Well. If they insisted.

He spun with it, came at his attacker with his own fist up, a knee for good measure that caught the fellow in the hip at the same time as a messy blow to the jaw. The man lost his grip, and Izzy laid into him quick, three shots to the chin and an uppercut that sent him reeling.

The other fool grabbed Izzy's shoulder and pulled him near, aiming no doubt to get a hand on his neck, not counting on Izzy to duck under his arm. To pivot. To come up under his chin with a hand clenched not in a boxer's fist but the blunt cat's-paw of a man fighting for his life.

Once, twice in the windpipe, and the bigger man fell back, clutching his neck. Before either of the brutes recovered, Izzy bolted. The savage in him had wanted to stay, get serious, deliver a proper lamming. As if those maggots were the source of all his woes. As if wounding them would change a thing. And so he ran, as he had before and would again.

When he reached streets he knew, he darted down a laneway and halted in the shadows. Fanned his own garments, making sure of his knife, his watch, the stiffly folded banknotes in various pockets. His hands hurt, and a few places on his body, as if he'd been struck and not noticed what with his thick coat and his tolerance for pain.

The sweat was cooling on him, and soon the night would get properly cold. It was already past the hour when Gummage locked the front door. Taking all caution, he sneaked through the quieting streets, keeping to shadows, hoping he looked like a threat and not fresh meat. At the corner of Renfield he was tempted to keep on, disguise his destination, but there was no one about and he was starting to shiver. The clack of his heels up the footpath made him wince, as did the squeak of the garden gate, but there stood the house, golden light shining behind the bubbled glass over the door.

Mrs. Gummage was herself, and he crept up to his cell grateful of its minor comforts. The dark. The quiet. The locked door. Alone, he was safe. Alone was better than dead.

A Bit of Leisure

Izzy wasn't merely alone, he was painfully lonesome. Lying in bed the next morning, trying to talk himself into getting up, he reckoned that he'd never gone so long without company. He had always had someone around: a brother, his mother, even Da grumbling in his chair. His old friends, one of whom was always ready for a gab, a wander round town. His new friends at the House. Noel. Here he had one mad old woman and a growing list of individuals to avoid.

Once he heard from Ursula's solicitor and got his accounts set up, he'd get into better lodgings. Possibly in a whole other house. There was something consumptive about the coughing from some of the other rooms. As a fresh round broke out to his right, he took it as a sign to get up and get on with his day.

Provisions would help. He hadn't seen a comb in days, never mind tooth powder. He roamed until he found a barbershop, the heat of the towels so soothing he near fell asleep in the middle of the shave. The barber directed him to a well-to-do department store, where he purchased a hat to replace the one lost last night. A wretched habit to adopt, losing hats while running for one's life, but at least he looked somewhat different. As well he laid in a good stock of grooming products, traveller's sized bottles of hair oil, neem oil, petroleum jelly (as if he'd a need, though it would do good to his wind-burnt lips), a brush and comb in a smart little case, a few sets of ready-made undergarments and a calfskin Gladstone to carry it all. Bless the clerk for not flinching when Izzy told him where to have the lot sent.

Pleased with himself, feeling too flush to go around the job shops, he meandered towards the riverfront, hoping for something interesting to observe. A ship being built, rare cargo offloading. Men, working on same. Men who wouldn't mind being watched.

The piers stood out into the broad river like long fingers. The general public could only get so close, but he found a fine vantage point at a broad gap between two buildings where the road took a sharp turn before descending to pier-side. Everywhere he looked was hectic activity, people of all sorts, all class and colour, hurrying to and fro with barrows and carts and tools and sheaves of paper, in and out of the brick offices and the grand warehouses standing proudly over them. Beyond stood the ships, outsizing all else, great moveable mountains of industry, their masts and spars clustered like bare branches in a winter wood.

He was not the only gawker, a number of other people standing about, men and women both. After a few minutes most moved on, save for one gent who now glanced

Izzy's way. On sensing Izzy's attention, he looked again, more directly. Then away.

Well. Likely nothing. A pity though, for the man had the look of good breeding and was dressed very finely. By the stars, Izzy was scum for real if he was this ready to abandon his spectacular promise to Noel. But he'd done no more than look, take in a pleasant sight on a dull day.

When he looked again, the fellow had moved in speaking distance, though he kept his gaze on the piers below. Clear of cheek, dark-eyed, he was a charmer for sure, if a touch too much like Izzy himself to be truly dazzling, with those hungry shadows around his eyes.

"Afternoon," Izzy said as the fellow looked his way. The most basic of acknowledgements. A word which meant nothing. The other man could pretend to have not even heard.

"A good day to you," he replied in a well-bred voice. He darted his tongue nervously over his lips. Or was that Izzy making too much of a careless gesture? "A fine day for a bit of leisure," the fellow said with another sideways glance.

Shit. As if his guts had ever guessed wrong. "Not to mince words, but I'm compelled to ask before we further our acquaintance what exactly your idea of leisure is." The other man froze, his face paling. With a strangled gasp he spun about and started up the street.

"Hang on, I ain't about to grass," Izzy called after him. "Don't run off, all right?" He ran the few steps to catch up with the man who waited with evident reluctance, his shoulders up around his ears, his eyes darting. "I'm no stranger to the trade, but you must be desperate, trying it on in broad daylight like this."

"I should have never spoken to you," the fellow muttered, his chin buried in his collar.

"Well, now you have. What's your name?"

"Why do you want to know?"

"So as I don't have to keep on calling you that chap what tried to hook me dockside." He'd meant to make light, but the other man flinched in something like pain. "Never mind, gov. Forget all that, hey? Not so long ago, I'd have jumped at the chance, a well-turned out sort like you."

"Do you mean this?" He gestured to his tailored frockcoat. "It's all I've got to my name, if you must know."

"No wonder you were on the trot."

"It wasn't for the money."

"Just the needing, hey?"

"By Jove, I'm a wretch," the man spat, making a dreadful face.

"We're none of us angels, friend. What's your name?"

"Charles. Charlie, if you please."

"Good to meet you, Charlie-if-you-please."

The man laughed dryly, his sore expression easing a touch. "And to whom do I owe the pleasure of nearly having solicited?"

Despite the candour of the moment, twenty-two years of healthy mistrust clamoured at Izzy to keep what protections he could. "I'm Peter." His brother's name. Noel's last name. Surely he'd remember. The other man took it as given, with a serious nod to match his strong handshake.

"So if you don't need the money, you must have work," Izzy said. "Or is this coat the bitter remains of your regal inheritance?"

He laughed again more easily. "So to speak. But yes, I've

work. Are you in need?"

"Is a man ever not?"

With Christmastime upon them, every grand home in the city was hosting a ball or fete or recital and in some cases all three in one night. There was hence an endless need of temporary servants: servers, cooks and cleaners, housemaids for houseguests and grooms to drive the carriages to and fro. Being adept at mixing drinks and putting up with aristocrats, Izzy was taken on as Charlie's second in the beverage service.

Many long, hectic, sticky, vaguely humiliating hours later, they turned in their hired jackets to the head of housekeeping, received what seemed a pittance in return though Izzy hadn't the mind to count it, and were sent on their way. He followed Charlie out into the night, not caring of the destination.

He wasn't used to being so comprehensively ignored, though the high-toned guests had plenty of interest in whatever was on the tray he'd been holding. Not a one of them had met his eye, even when they'd elbowed him, stepped on his toes, reached over his shoulder with their jewel-decked hand to snatch the last cup of fizzy wine. He'd got told off by the head butler for having too fierce an expression.

"How are you feeling?" Charlie said, falling into step with him.

"Like death walking. Do you seriously do that every night?"

"Every night I can."

"That's a wicked way to earn a living."

Charlie chuckled, hands deep in his pockets. "I've had it worse. At Kentley's you had to be up and dressed by six."

"Kentley? As in, Lord Edgar?"

"Second son of the Earl of Ridley? Dear me, did you work for him as well?"

"Made him work, more like."

"I don't understand," Charlie said, frowning hard.

"Lucky. With your looks, I'd have thought he'd have been all over you."

His shoulders up around his ears, Charlie didn't answer, which was itself an answer. He stopped at the next corner. "This is my street. Are you...well, what are you going to do? I've not much of a room but I've good whiskey."

More than his reluctance to be alone once more, the revelation about Kentley had goosed Izzy's curiosity. "I wouldn't mind a drink."

Charlie led the way up the grim alley, though the townhouse they entered seemed tidily kept. His upstairs room was larger than Izzy and Noel's in Charring Cross and better outfitted, with two chairs, a table, a tatted coverlet, everything as tidy as a butler's room ought to be.

"I know it's not much," Charlie confessed, putting his overcoat on a hanger.

"Cobber, compared to mine this is a palace." Izzy pulled out a chair and sat, groaning with relief. This had to be how Noel felt after a morning in the mud, as though one had been underfoot at a parade. He wriggled out of his own coat as Charlie took a pair of glasses and a tall bottle from a suitcase under the bed and poured them each a measure.

"When did you work for old Edgar?" he asked as Charlie took the other seat.

"Kentley? About a year and a half ago, I suppose. I barely lasted a fortnight. After what he did." He swallowed half his drink in one gulp and set the glass down hard. "By God, I'd never felt so irrelevant."

"He's a right shocker, ain't he? Liked to call me guttersnipe."

Charlie gasped, his hand trembling on the glass. "That's what he called me."

"It's not much of a compliment, I'll grant."

"You don't understand."

"No? Is it more of an insult when one has your better background?"

His face hardened. "That's not what I meant. He sacked another man named Charles to hire me."

"That's a rum coincidence."

"Coincidence? It was bloody well deliberate. So he didn't have to bother learning someone else's name." He snatched the bottle and poured, spilling a little on the table. "Lord above, he's a nightmare."

"Charles?"

"No, that beast Kentley. Charles is...he was my friend." His ire spent, he slumped on the table, propping his head in one hand, clutching the glass with the other. A mirror of Izzy's emotions, every time he thought of Noel.

"I'm sorry."

"He's not—" He caught himself, as if refusing to give voice to the fears. "I mean, I don't know what's happened to him. I haven't seen him in ages. I'm only sticking about because this was where we were last together. The only place I can think he'd come back to. I'm sorry, I shouldn't be saying all this to you."

"I understand. I have a friend worth waiting for." So why was he here with this man? Because the night was cold, the way was dark, the destination a misery. Because here it was warm and the door was locked and no one was trying to beat him or rob him or fool him. Because he didn't know how to be alone.

Time passed and the awkward silence became less so. The whiskey really was quite good, a proper drop, hinting of honey and old leather. Much more of it and he'd fall asleep in the chair. "So what's this friend of yours like?" Izzy asked, for want of something to rouse himself. "Must be quite something if you're putting up with all this in hopes of seeing him again."

Charlie laughed a little. "Charles? He was...he is a curious gent."

"Ain't we all. But I want to know. Slim, round, taller than you?"

"A shade shorter. Dark hair. Brown eyes." He paused, closed his eyes, swallowed hard. Smiled and went on. "He smokes too much, these awful smelly French cigarettes. And I think I might have ruined his life."

"That last one sounds familiar."

"You've ruined someone's life?"

"Perhaps."

"Someone you love?"

"Yeah, well, that's the bit that did the ruining, innit?"

Izzy drained his glass, didn't object when Charlie poured again. The whiskey had warmed their bodies and their bodies were warming the room. Charlie's cheeks were rosy as he lifted his foot onto the edge of his chair to untie his bootlace.

"I told you about Charles," he said. "Tell me how you met Kentley."

"Saints above, why do you want to know?"

"Because I'd like to understand. If you didn't work for him, how do you know him. How is it he called you rude names?"

He wanted not to say. Ought never to have mentioned Kentley at all, but his surprise had overcome good sense. Now he felt bound to a certain degree of honesty. "Just part of the job. Putting up with wealthy men running their fool mouths."

"Wealthy men? What are you, some kind of journeyman domestic?"

"As in going house to house? Nah, they came to me."

"For what?" The lamb hadn't a clue, goggling at Izzy, his forehead screwed.

"To get put to work. Serving me."

His eyes grew wide. He opened and closed his mouth a few times. Izzy said nothing, rolling the whiskey in his glass, waiting for Charlie to decide how deep the offense.

"Tell me what you did to Kentley," he said at last in a thin voice.

"Why do you want to know?"

"Because I'd like to imagine him suffering."

"I did my best to make that happen, rest assured."

"Tell me. Did you beat him."

"Of course."

"Tie his hands, tie him to things?"

"You seem to know a lot about this."

Charlie sat back, breathing hard, his face redder than ever. "I can hardly help it, after what he had me do. Tell me what you did to him."

"No. You've got a mind, you've got knowledge of him, figure it for yourself. I'm for home." Leaving the dregs, feeling every bit he'd drank, Izzy stood. He tried to take his coat, but it was caught on the corners of the chair back. He got it free, turned to find Charlie barring his way.

"Please stay," he gasped. "Whatever you want, I'll do."

"That's an awful lot to offer, cobber."

Charlie shuddered, choking on his words. "You don't understand how I need this. I've been by myself so long, I've started to question if I'm even alive. If this is truly my life, or just some dream from which I can't ever wake."

Izzy's turn to shiver, to hear his own most secret and terrifying fear spoken by another, that none of this was real. Worse, that this was all there was, this dirty life of labour and self-loathing, and Noel and Ursula and everything good he'd ever known were mere figments of his imagination. He was starting to crack and he'd only been gone a week. How long had Charlie waited for his love? Ages, to judge from the longing in his eyes, the tremble of his hand laid on Izzy's chest.

"Please, don't leave me with this feeling. I can pay you," he added when Izzy didn't answer.

"That don't amount, cobber."

"Then what is it you want?"

"Not to break my promises." He stepped back but Charlie intercepted him again, grabbing his arm fiercely.

"Please don't leave. I'll do whatever you ask."

"In that case, let me go." Charlie's grip was strong, not to be loosed without wrenching effort. He was taller than Izzy, heavier of build, mad with grief and drink, looming over him with dark intent in his eyes. Another betrayer, in which case Izzy was safer alone. "I said let me go, or I'll smash your face in, you drunken arsehole."

He spoke quietly but the words struck hard. Charlie gasped, blinked as if waking. He let Izzy go and sat heavily on the bed, staring at his hands. "Oh God. What was I thinking?"

"You weren't thinking at all. Which is why I'm off."

"I'm sorry."

"I'm sure you are." He let himself out. As he closed the door, he heard Charlie begin to sob. Despite the softness in him that wanted to comfort the fool, the sense in him knew where that led, to the very thing he'd just evaded. One more man about town Izzy couldn't wholly trust. One more reason this whole scheme was madness. Having RPA up his arse couldn't be nearly as torturous as this death by a thousand heartbreaks, to be endured alone.

NOEL

He woke feeling less fragile and pledging to not drink tonight, fed up with feeling like his guts were inside out. Charlie had offered similar work if he was to go round his flat by one in the afternoon. Having nothing else, heartsick at the thought of another lonesome day and empty evening, Izzy struck out from the Manse around noon.

Passing along the populous high street, beset by a thousand voices and faces and not one of them someone he wished to see, his aloneness stalked him like a foul shadow, inescapable. By the stars, it was turning his head already. He was at most a day's train ride from home. A letter he sent today would be in Ursula's hands tomorrow. He ought to write one, as chances were she'd not heard about the fire at the bawdy.

He got directions to the post office, where he bought paper and a pencil and stood by the corner of the long counter to write:

Maam,

Yor frends moved house no forward address - Have you other connexions? Still not heard from yor agent here - am at loose ends. Any replie send to my logings.

For nearly a minute he debated asking about Noel, but the fewer clues he left the better, and he merely added a line that he wished them all well. If something happened, Ursula would find a way to let him know.

The evening's work passed in the same exhausting blur. Clod-footed, indifferent, he ended up at Charlie's flat again, where the other man drank himself into a similar stupor as the night before and Izzy drank nothing.

After an hour, he'd had his fill of the maudlin company. Charlie was friendly enough and had clearly been brought up well, but whatever had steered him off his steady path had exacted a heavy toll, made him prone to melancholy, worsened by the drink. There went Izzy himself, if he wasn't careful.

It was past one in the a.m. and Charlie was well out of it, his head laid on his folded arms on the table, but when Izzy stood, he startled upright.

"Are you leaving?" he asked, rubbing his eyes.

"I'm bushed. You are too, by the looks of you."

"I do wish you'd stay."

"It's best I don't."

"I'm sorry about last night."

"I know you are. Or I'd have stayed away entirely," Izzy said kindly as he put on his overcoat. "You ought to get some sleep. You'll fall apart, going on this way."

Toying with his empty glass, Charlie only nodded, and

Izzy let himself out. It was snowing again, hard flakes that struck his face like thrown sand, borne by a wicked wind. The journey back to what barely passed as home took on a sinister caste, evidence of his ruin confronting him at every turn. Beggars and bullies loomed at him from stinking alleys, hard-eyed molls called from shadowed doorways, and always there was the sound of someone crying: a child, a dog, a woman. What had been the point in saving his life if this was all he gained, this meagre survival and a bitter, unavoidable notion that he might have been better off dead.

And yet when a looming figure came at him from the black corner of the Manse's front garden, all his woes were not enough to keep his heart from wanting to keep on beating. He leapt back with a snarl, fists at the ready. "By God, I've had it with this poxy fucking town. If you want at me, you Mersey piece of shit, come on then."

"For fuck's sake, Pound, keep it down," the figure hissed.

Peters.

Noel.

Noel, stepping into the light, grey-faced, shaking with cold. Noel, in the flesh, alive and well, and Izzy grabbed him to prove he was real and not a cruel vision.

"Saints above, Noel…"

"Am I ever glad to see you," he stammered.

"You frightened me out of my wits."

"You think you're frightened?"

"I ain't no more." Izzy could have scaled a mountain, fought a legion. Couldn't stop grinning. "Why are you out here freezing your arse off, you twit?"

"I went for tea, and when I came back she'd locked the door."

"She'd have let you in."

"Yeah, well there were some hard types hanging about. I've had a hell of a time already."

"Never mind that, let's get you inside."

Mrs. Gummage answered cheerily, smelling of sherry. "I wondered where this one had got to," she said with a nod towards Noel. "He were waiting hours for you."

"I had work," Izzy replied. "Is there a room for Mr. Peters?"

"You've taken the last, I'm afraid. But you're both lean enough lads. I'm sure you can cram." She laughed her tinkling laugh, setting her necklaces swinging, then shuffled off.

"I guess that's that. Come on." Izzy started up the stairs.

"What'd she mean by cram?" Noel asked as he followed.

"It's close quarters. We'll have to stack."

Noel chuckled. "Sounds good. I ain't never been so cold."

"Do you not have a coat?"

"I'm wearing it."

"First thing tomorrow, we'll kit you out. And get looking for a better room. I wasn't joking about the stacking."

"What d'you mean?"

"Just...duck your head going in," Izzy said, unlocking his door. He opened it and gestured for Noel to precede him.

Noel peered in. "This is it?"

"It's this or the shrubbery out front."

"Fair enough." He went in and sat on the bed. Izzy

remained in the doorway where he blocked most of the light from the hall.

"Shall I give you the grand tour? We've got a floor and ceiling and everything."

Noel chuckled, bending to unlace his boots. "Save it for later."

"Sorry I can't offer more."

"It's enough." He sat up, set his hands on his knees and looked Izzy over. "Am I ever glad to see you."

"Likewise."

Seconds passed in silence. From hellish misery to the heights of paradise was a dizzying ascent, and Izzy's mind hadn't quite caught up with the physical fact of Noel's presence. In part as he could barely see him, the tiny room a chamber of shadows, Noel little more than a gleam of eyes and grinning teeth.

"You really going to stand there staring after I've come all this way for you?"

"For me?"

"Who else, you daft bugger?"

"One doesn't like to presume. I sort of thought you might hate me."

Noel laughed again kindly. "How could I ever hate you?"

"Because I ran off. Left you to deal with everything."

"You did what you had to. And I'm here, ain't I?"

"And I can hardly believe it."

"Come. Sit." Noel touched the place beside him.

"Hold that thought." Izzy backed out of the room, felt his way to the WC. Shut himself into the narrow booth. Leaned against the back of the door and let go of the tears he'd been holding. The emotion in him had no name, was a fullness in his chest and a chill in his guts and a sense that if Noel had come all this way, he wasn't merely running to Izzy but running away from everything else.

Or Izzy had gone right out of his head, and the room was empty. No, he'd touched Noel. Mrs. Gummage had seen him. Izzy wasn't mad. He went back to his room. Paused before the closed door. If he was dreaming...

He took a deep breath. Shivered as he caught the scent of Noel hanging in the air. He opened the door.

RUINED

HE'D HAD A DUTY, had he not? To make sure Izzy was safe. To confirm in the flesh. It didn't mean that Noel was weak. That Izzy's absence made him feel less than a man. Only, Izzy's presence made Noel so much more.

Ursula ought to be glad of having one less soul to save. Glad too of not being able to say precisely where he'd gone, in case Everley or the royal pain came calling. She'd forgive him. Noel had told himself this time and again on the northbound train. Otherwise he'd have fallen to thinking about the card that curly-haired lord had given him, his storied name and Marylebone address embossed on the front, *jobs avail* pencilled on the back. Domestic service, which for Noel would mean scullery at best, more likely garden or stable. Legal, dull, frightening in its appeal.

He was a fool if he thought it would make him happier. Eloise, Prue, Brigid, Honey: all had left exploitive service jobs to work at the House, the stories they told of randy masters and punitive housekeepers the stuff of penny-dreadfuls. Sir Sideburns (for Noel had blanked the man's name from his mind) might well want him for a pet. Double labour, a single wage, and a miserable one at that by all accounts. Shovelling all day, whippings all night. Precisely the sort of life he wished to transcend.

That night, Noel had shut himself in his and Izzy's room and thought through every scenario, every path down which his life might go. The lord's offer barely rated, except as a last resort. Noel could stay where he was, take his chances alongside Ursula and the rest. Try to ignore the empty bed. But there was no dodging Muldoon. The snare was set, and they were rabbits being driven toward it. Or he could go north. Find Izzy. Whatever was coming, they'd do better together.

He left the following morning without stopping to tell anyone. Ursula would have fussed over him, tried to dissuade, offered a chaperone. On his own, Noel could move faster, change his mind on the instant, follow his instincts and not the directives of another. If conditions were bad, he wanted to have to mind only himself.

Time went on, measured in stops, the sky like slate, rain hanging over the hills in grey sheets. Leaving the train, Noel felt eyes upon him. Leaving the station, the feeling grew, but that might have been the cold, or his growing awareness of the sheer illogic of his plan. Yes, he was here, and so was Izzy, but so were half a million other souls, not one of whom cared if he lived or died.

Nervy, shivering, conspicuously from elsewhere, he crept around town in ever widening circuits, seeking Renfield Lane. Was there a risk in asking about the Manse? Was it itself a whorehouse or merely a flophouse? A secret or a given? He knew nothing, dared nothing, too nervous to eat, too cold to stop moving.

Rose had however been right, by the first glance he knew he'd found it, for every other building on the row was a hovel beside its grand proportions. Mrs. Gummage was friendly enough, letting him wait in the musty dining room. After a few hours, sick with hunger and bored beyond belief, Noel had gone out to find a meal. Gotten lost on his way back, alarmed by how swiftly dark fell, his every horror coming true, that this had been a fool's errand, a disaster in the making. Made real, as he found the Manse's door locked.

To knock was to draw to himself the sort of attention he had spent all day avoiding. That frail lady had like as not gone to bed, and the door would be answered by some brute who'd send Noel packing. He didn't even know what name Izzy was under. If any, for the Manse was a transient's lodgings, populated by ragged men with no better address and possibly strong desires to remain unknown.

And so Noel had waited in the front garden, as the chill crept into his bones and his heart, as he began to wonder if Izzy was already back and he'd missed him by leaving. Midnight came with a tolling of bells and a ill wind that had forced Noel into the lee of the house. By the time his mark came hurrying up the footpath, he was nearly too cold to move.

And now this terrible room, and Izzy terrified, and Noel laughing to himself at how wrong things could go even when one tried to do right.

He lit the bit of candle, then undressed and got into the

bed. There was nowhere else to be, and like as not undressing with another body in the room would end in one of them taking an elbow to the head. Absurd conditions, this miserable closet in a mouldering house in a filthy town too far from home. So why was Noel smiling?

The reason opened the door and slipped into the room, the gust of closing the door making the candle gutter. Izzy paused, taking in the sight of Noel under the blankets but clearly unclothed. Waiting.

"Thought I'd save us some time," Noel said. "You all right?"

Izzy was down to his shirtsleeves. Moving slowly, he hung his outerwear over the foot of the bed. "I was afraid I'd dreamt you. It's been a rough few days."

"It's been a nightmare, it has. You wouldn't believe what's gone on since you left."

"Is that why you're here?"

"It's why I scarpered in such a hurry. But I'm here for you."

"What happened?"

"Don't make me tell you now. Just come to bed."

"But—"

"The trouble will keep till tomorrow, Pound. I need you now." He shifted to one side, flipped back the blankets. "Come on, get cracking. Mr. Peters didn't come all this way for nothing."

There, Izzy's crooked smile, the one that made Noel's heart leap. "Fucking hell, did I ever miss you."

"Come here and prove it."

Still slow, as if Noel might dissipate like mist if he moved too quickly, Izzy came around the foot of the bed, sat down on the edge. Noel sat up and tried to take his hand but he drew back.

"What's wrong?" he asked.

"I want to say I'm sorry."

"I thought you hated that word."

"Yeah, but I really mean it this time. I'm sorry for having dragged you down."

"What are on about?"

"Once upon a time, there you were, minding your own business. Then I came along, and that was it. Ruined." Izzy was trembling, his voice was thick as if he might start to cry, his misery stabbing at Noel's heart.

"You mustn't think like that. It's too late, first of all. And second, it was worth it to have you to love."

Izzy frowned, as if unable to grasp the notion that he could be worth anything at all. "But I ruined your life!" he protested.

"You didn't. I promise. And I swear, I'd do it all over the same again. Make the same choices, if that's what puts me right here. With you." He took Izzy's hand and held on when he would have pulled away. Waited for that blessed, crooked smile Noel loved to hell and back.

"Can you believe I thought I could live without you?" Izzy croaked, rubbing at his tears.

"Actually I do. That's exactly the sort of foolish thing you'd think."

Izzy gaped at him. Then he laughed for real, a proper, gleeful, Izzy kind of laugh, loud enough to set their nearest neighbour pounding on the wall for silence.

"You did what you thought best," Noel whispered, squeezing Izzy's hand. "You tried to spare me. But we're better off together."

"I know that now."

"And don't forget it, you twit. Now strip off and get in bed, quick smart."

"I don't know what you expect we're going to achieve," Izzy said as he began to unbutton his shirt.

"You leave that to me." Because he was having Izzy, here and now. And Izzy was mighty loud. But he was smiling, and it was glorious, and nothing in the world could stop them.

My Man

TOGETHER. AT LAST AND for always together, his wretched past of no account, his future made for loving Noel. Noel, embracing him, tugging at his collar, kissing his neck. Noel, touching Izzy's cheek, kissing him and kissing him, and sweet mercy, it felt so good he nearly wept.

"You all right?" Noel asked, pulling back to let him breathe.

"I'm grand. I've missed you so."

"I love you."

Such a joy to hear those words from this man's mouth. "I'm never leaving you again."

Noel smiled, full of glory. "As if I'd let you."

"Do you mean that?"

"I do. It's you and me, from here on."

They kissed again, all tenderness, but not nearly enough. He twisted from Noel's grasp then stood up cautiously to pull off his shirt, which he tossed over the end of the bed. Dropping his trousers caused a gust that blew out the candle.

"Forget about it," he chuckled. "As if I'm gonna get lost in here." The little chamber wasn't even as dark as their room at the House, and Noel was so near Izzy could feel the heat of him against his bare legs. Hands outstretched, he moved carefully, but the second his knees touched the mattress, Noel grabbed his arms and pulled him on top.

He'd doffed the blanket, and his bare skin seared against Izzy's, the scent of him everywhere, his hands as well, up and down Izzy's back, grasping at his buttocks, promising everything. Practical considerations loomed: the challenge of keeping quiet, the narrowness of the bed, the lack of grease to make their goal achievable.

"I've got nothing for it," he whispered as Noel prised him open with his spit-wet fingers.

"I've had you before without."

"Usually because it's our second go and you've spent in me already."

Noel shivered, always stirred by such bodily facts. "That's unfair."

"Facts of life."

"Then again, maybe that means we've got our solution at hand." He rolled to spill Izzy off him, nearly tipping him onto the floor. His yelp earned them another thumping on the wall from their neighbour. Snorting with the effort not to laugh, obeying Noel's touches and whispered directives even as he wondered what he was playing at, Izzy got on the bed on his hands and knees.

"This ain't gonna wo—oh, fucking hell..."

Work. It wouldn't work if Noel thought he could go charging in. That's not what he was doing. What he was doing was stroking Izzy's prick, with a close, insistent grip. Professional almost, the touch of a man with serious intentions. Hips twitching, Izzy swore again. So did their neighbour, the poor man, whose bed must have been against the shared wall.

"Keep quiet, scum," Noel hissed. The filthy word struck Izzy as it always did, and he groaned as he arched into Noel's grip. "I said quiet." Noel let up his stroking, but only to push Izzy's head down. There was the sound of a tongue, then with a slick hand he recommenced working Izzy's prick.

"What are you even after?" Izzy panted.

"Cream. Yours."

"You filthy fucker!"

"If we're lucky. Tell me when."

"Mercy, can't be long."

"Shut up and spill it for me. You must be bursting. Aching for me to fill—"

"Now, now!" He was everything Noel said: bursting, aching, ready to give his all, and he bit his own arm to keep from shouting aloud as he spent, Noel's other hand cupped over the end of his prick to catch his gushing.

"That ought to do," Noel growled. Leaving Izzy's prick hanging, slightly stinging, his head singing, Noel slathered his handful over Izzy's hole. Worked it in, as Izzy spread for it, desperate and desperately curious. It felt right, felt easy, felt just like he wanted, Noel's fingers sliding around and around and in.

"Stop me if you have to."

"Never stop."

"I wish. I wish I could do nothing but this. Love you like

this forever."

Love, in the form of Noel's prick sliding between Izzy's slick buttocks, seeking perfect and unlawful union. Love, in the tremble of Noel's hands, sticky on Izzy's thighs, his back, his arse, coaxing him to tilt his hips just so. Love, in the fact that Noel had crossed the nation to be here to do these things to him, to love him this way, never to stop, never to leave him.

If they moved too quickly, the bed squeaked something awful. There was no place else to be, and so they moved slowly, saying nothing, Noel not thrusting but flowing, over and into and out of him, like waves falling on a hard shore. Noel's climax was a series of taut twitches and a choked back groan, his fingers digging into Izzy's hips.

He withdrew, stood up, swore heartily as his head made contact with the wall. Sat down on the bed again, clutching his forehead. "You're shitting me."

"I ought to have warned you," Izzy said as he shifted over to give Noel room to lie down. "Damn near broke my nose, first morning."

"We're clearing out of here tomorrow," Noel murmured.

"A-fucking-men to that."

Right beside him, their neighbour bashed on the wall again. "Will you two fookin' fairies shut th' bloody hell up and go to fookin' sleep already?"

IZZY HAD A MOMENT of pure panic on waking to find himself pressed to the wall with a man's arm around him.

But the arm was brown, and the man was Noel, and the relief was near orgasmic.

With much caution, he clambered over Noel, got into his shirt, and scurried to the WC. With luck the wash room was also vacant and he did what he could with only cold water and no towel. When he got back, Noel was awake and was dressing in the square of space at the foot of the bed. "This is miserable. How long did you intend on stopping here?"

"Truth is I've been so bushed I hardly noticed."

"How have you been spending your days?"

"Looking for work, finding trouble. Met a man who worked for Kentley."

"Saints preserve us."

There was a knock at the door. Noel clammed up as Izzy cracked it open a sliver, but it was Mrs. Gummage, weighed down on one side by Izzy's new Gladstone. "It were too late last night to be bringing this up," she said.

"Thank, I forgot I'd bought it."

"There's this as well," she said. She began searching the pockets of her brightly patterned robe, then stopped, one finger raised in realization. She batted away the necklaces to extract an envelope from her loose bodice.

"Ah. Thanks so much," he said holding the warm paper by one corner.

"And about your guest—"

"We'll be seeking elsewhere for lodgings. No offence to yourself, ma'am. You run a very clean house."

"No offence taken. You clearing out spares me no end of palaver with John Law." Snickering, she toddled away.

"What's all that?" Noel asked as Izzy closed the door.

"Change of clothes. The letter, I don't know." It was addressed to E.P. c/o U. Barkley. Ursula's married name, told to him in absolute confidence the day he'd left.

"What's it say?"

"Hang on, I'm getting to that." The letter was addressed directly to him, much it seeming to be about kind regards and the weather at this time of year. He began to pick through it for useful words. "Here we are. Something, something, present yourself at the offices to obtain access to your account."

"What are they on about?"

"It's from Ursula. I've credit now."

"Credit?"

"Off my gratuities. She had a hundred and twenty odd quid squirreled away on my behalf. "

"Fucking hell, Pound! I thought I made out well."

"Yeah, well, we're making out like princes today. Clean underwear and everything." They dressed with care, packing everything into the valise and taking it with them. Thence to the barber shop, to emerge with shining cheeks and primped hair and a great improvement in both odour and attitude.

The solicitor's office was in a grand building with stone lions guarding its green marble steps and a chandelier fit for a ballroom hanging in the lobby. The law office was equally impressive, panelled where it wasn't lined with bookshelves, all of it as comforting as it was off-putting and smelling strongly of furniture polish. Ursula's business was evidently well protected.

Holding the valise, Noel stayed by the door as Izzy approached the tidy clerk behind the desk, his very best accent at the ready. "I've been asked to present myself to your offices," he said, passing over the letter.

The clerk took it in his long fingers and read over it swiftly. "Very good, Mr. Pound. Lord Ingleby will need your signature on a few documents." He returned the letter and stood up. "If you'd like to have a seat, I shall see if he's free at the moment. Your man may wait in the lobby."

"I'm sorry, are you referring to Mr. Peters?"

The clerk paused, glanced at Noel. Izzy smiled, a politely threatening grin he'd put much effort into while working out his headmaster's routine. "Mr. Peters is not my *man*. He is my associate. He'll wait right here."

The clerk did some swift calculation, eyes darting between them. Then he resumed his placid smile. "Ah. Yes. My mistake."

"Don't let it trouble you."

Blushing right up the back of his neck, the clerk hurried away. Izzy sat on the plush leather sofa and beckoned for Noel to join him.

"Thanks for that," he murmured. "Not that I'd have minded."

"I would have. My man indeed. The bleeding nerve." He left unmentioned his gut-wrenching terror at the thought of Noel being so far away.

The clerk returned quickly with tea for them both. Some minutes later, he brought Izzy into the other office, where the bewhiskered solicitor made small talk about London weather while the clerk whisked about with the papers, putting them under first the solicitor's pen then Izzy's. They gave him ten pounds, and instructions on how to bill against his account being held by their southern branch, as if he were a rich man's son being obliged to manage his own affairs for the first time.

Soon enough he and Noel were back outside. "So now what?" Noel asked, hunching his shoulders as the wind caught him.

"Now we get you a proper coat. Then lunch. Then I say we find a hotel." Izzy started walking and Noel fell into step beside.

"A hotel? For what?"

"For staying at, you berk."

"That's a waste of money, innit, when we ought to be looking for something long term?"

"Let's live a little. I thought I was going to die without ever seeing you again. I'd like to celebrate that not having happened. Come on, a nice big room with a steaming bath, we'll have dinner brought up. I'll have my man give me a rub-down, we'll have a lovely evening."

Noel chuckled past his shivering. "Your man? I thought I was your associate."

"Associate, apprentice, man. Husband."

"Sounds like I'm all things to all people."

"No. Just to me."

"Always."

PEELERS

ONE STEP INTO THE lobby, Noel knew they'd chosen wrong. It was too nice a hotel for them, no matter how much money they were prepared to spend. Every eye was upon them, the ladies peering down their noses, some gents openly staring, including the clerks at the reception desk.

"Are you sure this is wise?" he murmured to Izzy, one pace ahead.

"Nonsense, Peters," Izzy replied loudly in his fanciest speech. "I'm certain there'll be a vacancy."

Peters. So he was to play Izzy's 'man' after all. He'd forgive him if he pulled this off, as the hotel was proper luxury, all glittering glass and sleek tiles and palms in pots. He was carrying the valise, and at a glance from Izzy he paused and let his 'employer' approach the long desk.

There was some back and forth, then Izzy laughed, a falsely merry sound. "I see the confusion. While Mr. Peters is indeed my secretary, I will be needing him far too frequently for him to be running back and forth from the servants' rooms."

The clerk blanched, his eyes contritely lowered. Izzy signed the register with a flourish, and the clerk summoned a boy to show them to their room on the third floor. It was a generous suite, with a grand canopied bed, a conversation set, and a little round dining table with a pair of chairs. A much smaller chamber adjoined, containing only a plain bed-stand, for servants who needed to be at hand.

At the door, Izzy tipped the boy a pair of coins that made the lad's eyes pop. "Thank you, sir," he stammered, bobbing his head. "If there's anything at all you need, you have only to ask for me. The name's Lennox. I'll do all I can to help."

"Much obliged, my good man. You could start by obtaining me some brandy. And for my secretary as well."

"Yes, sir. Straight away, sir. Sir," he said, nodding to Noel as well before he hastened away.

Izzy shut the door. Locked it. Leaned against it and sighed. "That ought to have been easier. Sorry I've had to lie about you. Again."

"Well, I am your associate," Noel said, shrugging out of his coat.

"But you're not my secretary."

"I could be, if you had a proper job."

"You could be my booking manager. You've got the savvy."

"That would make me your pimp."

Izzy laughed, ran his fingers through his hair with a groan of satisfaction. "Pimps are arseholes. Booking manager sounds pure class."

"So what's that make Ursula?"

"Her? She's an entrepreneuse."

The brandy arrived with a pair of fine glasses. Izzy asked about bathing and was directed to the sparkling clean men's facility at the end of the hall, with several shower spigots and a pair of deep tubs which Izzy claimed rivalled those at his beloved tennis club. Squeaky clean, they went back in the room, toasted their good fortune, and fucked until dinner time.

Quietly, though. Far more freely than in that coffin of a room at the Manse the night before, but still quiet, in whispers, murmurs, signals, their sounds of passion muffled by a hand, a forearm, the pillow, the mattress. The furniture was as solid as it appeared, at least every bit of it they tested, even the shabbier bed in the maid's room, which Izzy suggested as a way to prove both beds had been occupied.

Dinner was roast beef, and they dressed long enough for the food to be delivered. Then undressed to eat it, another suggestion of Izzy's, in the name of keeping their clothing tidy.

"That's the worst excuse they'll have ever heard for finding two naked men in a room together," Noel said as he stepped out of his trousers.

"Don't get entirely naked, in that case," Izzy said, pulling up his chair to the laden table. He was down to underclothes, one of his new sets, its fine fabric clinging to his chest in a most distracting manner.

Baffled by the rise of his prick after the previous hours' activities, Noel took his own seat across. "Be sensible."

"Pfft. If we were properly sensible, we wouldn't be here at all. But figs to that." Izzy raised his glass, the wine glowing in the wavering light. "Here's to you and to me and to no one bloody else. Not tonight, at any rate. They can take care of themselves for a change."

"I'll drink to that."

They drank, they ate, they quietly caroused. Having exhausted their first desperate urges, they spent much of the evening lying in each other's arms, talking, sometimes kissing, often simply gazing at each other, until one or the other would look away, overcome with emotion. They fell asleep like this. In the night, Noel awoke and got up to turn off the light fixture, which was still burning brightly overhead. Feeling his way back in the dark, he knocked his toes on a chair leg, biting back his curses as he hopped to bed. He laid down and Izzy rolled over, feeling for him under the covers.

"Did I wake you?" Noel whispered.

"I forgive you," Izzy murmured. He shifted nearer, rested his chin on Noel's shoulder, holding his hand where it lay between them. "Mmm. You're warm." He wriggled closer, his rising prick brushing Noel's fingers.

"And you're a fiend."

Izzy hummed a little laugh, tilting his hips away. "Sorry. Unless..." and he tilted forward, pressing against Noel again.

He lifted his hand away. "Save it, you flirt."

"Sorry."

"I thought you hated that word."

Izzy laughed dreamily again. "It didn't used to mean as much."

"Go to sleep, all right?"

"Yes, Mr. Peters." Izzy's grip was already slack, his breathing slowing.

Though Noel expected to lay awake fretting until dawn, when the weight of sleep descended he was smart enough to surrender. Regardless, he woke as early as ever, barely half six by the watch in Izzy's waistcoat hanging on the back of a chair.

He pushed open the drapes enough to set about tidying up. Sure, there were maids, but the room was in far too evident a state of male debauch, clothing dropped here and there, the remains of the dinner left to spoil, the open jar of jelly prominent on the night stand.

He screwed the lid on the jar, and went to put it away in the case in Izzy's bag, standing open on the luggage rack by the room door. There was quite the ruckus in the corridor given the early hour, and Noel peeped out through the little lens in the back of the door to spy a grim faced hotel clerk and a pair of blue-jackets coming towards him.

Never was a man so fleet of foot, as Noel spun about and leapt for the bed. "Pound, for the love of God, wake up!" he hissed, whipping the covers off to stir him faster.

"Hhnghh...you wha'?"

"Bleeding peelers out there!"

Izzy struggled upright, his hair a snarl. "Wha's got to do with us?"

The answer came in a solid thumping on their door. Grabbing up what seemed most like his own clothes, Noel dove for the tiny maid's room.

"What in blazes," Izzy shouted, falling into character. "Peters, did you hear that? I say, Peters, my good man."

You shit... "Sorry, sir, did you call me?" he yelled back.

"Never mind, I'll see to it myself." Grumbling, Izzy stomped to the door as the knocking came again. "Now that will be just about enough of that!"

The clerk said something inaudible and Izzy answered. They went back and forth while Noel dressed, though he had Izzy's too-small trousers and only one sock. It seemed not to matter, as Izzy was giving no ground and hadn't even opened the door.

"Now look," he said at last, in what Noel thought of as his Kentley voice, all chest and bravado. "This is the outside of enough. You've woken me up hours before I've requested with some utterly insulting nonsense, not to mention the affronting presence of two of Liverpool's finest, whom I'm sure have much better tasks at hand than answering this slanderous summons. You will remove yourselves from my door at once unless you care to show me verified cause to enter."

There seemed no answer, and Noel was steeling himself to leave his lowly refuge when Izzy came in, shaking all over. "We're clearing out of this poxy palace. More trouble than it's worth," he spat.

"Too right. I died a thousand deaths when I saw that lot in the corridor."

"Bless you for being awake to see them."

"Bless you for putting on a show just now."

"Yeah, well, this whole city's put me in a devil of a mood." Izzy turned, stumbled on his own heel, fetched up against the wall. "Shit. And I was having the nicest dream." He was trying to make light, but as his voice cracked Noel reached out and he went into his arms. "Is it too much to bleeding well ask, to get treated decently, just once? Not to have fight every cursed time for a shred of respect?"

"Forget it, Pound."

"I can't! I want to know who in hell did that to us, so I can pull his heart out and stomp it."

"You got to give it up. It don't matter."

"It bleeding well should. That should be the damned crime, ruining a man." He raised his head from Noel's shoulder, wiped his bleary eyes. "Ah well. If they don't want our scandalous money, we'll go spend it elsewhere."

"Yes, sir, Mr. Pound."

Izzy cocked an eyebrow at him. "What was that for?"

"Am I not your secretary? Disrespectful, innit, to call you otherwise?"

"Too true, Peters, too true." Smirking, he made to step back, but Noel pulled him close again. "What is it?"

"Just this." Just a kiss, while they were as close as they got to safe. One last kiss, in this dark, stale servant's room, before they dragged themselves out into the blinding light of all the world's denial and disgust. A kiss in place of all else Noel would give the man he loved: his heart, his life, his everything.

Mrs. Owen

If a doctor had told Ursula she was dying, she would have believed him without reservation. Lately she hurt everywhere, inside and out, body and soul, from the moment of waking until dropping into a laudanum-hazed bout of unconsciousness that never lasted long enough to leave her rested.

The disasters were legion, unending, consuming her days, breaking her heart. The meeting with the Admiral had gone poorly to say the least, the old sod stammering under his stiff upper lip until she left in disgust, though she had gone to him quite prepared to offer significant favours.

With Izzy's safe haven in the north gone, Noel had disappeared in pursuit. She'd had no word from him, or Marisol for that matter, who hadn't been seen by anyone in weeks. Prue's father was dying, Eloise's daughter had the mumps, and Muldoon was making near daily visits, typically just before the custom, as though it were his duty to inspect the House.

Meanwhile, other houses had begun to fall to the strange conspiracy, women arrested by the score, obliged to prove their nationality, condemned of far worse than indecency if they weren't British. What establishments survived the raids, Muldoon had claimed. The very last thing in the world that Ursula therefore wanted or needed was to come into her office that afternoon and find Mrs. Owen in tears.

She nearly turned on her heel and left the room. Whatever she was about to learn would only increase her suffering. But she owed so much to this brave woman. Her very life, in truth. Ursula drew a chair close and sat while Mrs. Owen blew her nose. Never a slender woman, Mrs. Owen strongly resembled her daughter Rose, with the same rich complexion, proud chin, round nose, bounteous bosom. For years she had operated an independent house by Leicester Square which Ursula had inherited as her only condolence from her bigamist husband. He'd left all the honourable parts of his substantial estate to his English wife.

Together Ursula and Mrs. Owen had reformed the staff, and the clientele. Eliminated all signs of pox and implemented obsessive standards. Survived a dozen police raids, and fended off three smash-and-grab attacks by local hooligans. One of the thugs Ursula had crippled for life with a blow of her cane which had shattered his ankle. His fault for attempting to molest her, and she'd been given wide berth from then on, even more once Lord Bolton became a known associate. If Mrs. Owen was rattled, then all was about to collapse.

"First, is it you who's in trouble?" Ursula asked.

Mrs. Owen shook her head. "Never mind me. Have you not heard what's happening?"

"So much is happening of late. Have the police been?"

"Forget the coppers, it's the city manager's men what be giving me the problems. We've been condemned."

"As what?"

"See, that's what I said, and the fellow gave me such a look, then gave me this great slapping letter." She gave Ursula a sheaf of documents, all painfully official, the seal of London taking up nearly half of the first page. "They're knocking down the whole row. Driving everyone out. They say the building's unfit for occupancy."

It shall be further incumbent upon owners of said properties to recompense the City Treasury for all works performed. Whereby any owner is unable to cover said aforementioned costs, the property shall become forfeit to the City Treasury, with all costs of said transfer to be added to any debt remaining...

A smash and grab. Knocking down the building, then extorting her for the costs. Ursula flicked through the pages, the words blurring, all of them horrible. No refuge, no recourse. The papers slid from her hand. Nothing mattered. A wind seemed to strike her, and the fetid stench of the pier, and for a moment she was her wretched young self, just off the boat from Norway, freshly widowed and thoroughly betrayed.

That night she did not open the House. Not wanting to forgo the income, they had been conducting business as usual, though the gaiety was somewhat forced and she had fielded many complaints about the absence of the boys. There was now no reason to please the clients. Muldoon could steal ashes.

And so she did not open the House. Sent Clyde out to mark the door with chalk, the sign for the clients to not bother trying their keys. Laid on her bed for a sleepless but silent hour as the staff arrived. They were assembled in the salon when she came downstairs. Prue and Eloise were absent, as she expected. Mrs. Owen and Rose sat together, Rose's eyes red, her face blank. All the rest were drawing off their anguish, and it was a muted and expectant audience that Ursula faced.

"I won't mince words," she said. "We haven't time, to be honest. It's possible, indeed, probable, that we will not be opening again."

"Of course not tonight," Annie started.

"I mean ever." Silence fell, as if all were holding their breath. Waiting for her to explain. "I must confess to having kept other matters from you, as I hoped they would pass us over."

"If it's about the raids that have been going on, there's not a moll in town that don't know about that," Sophie said tiredly.

"There's more of which I have just now learned. Mrs. Owen has informed me that the Leicester house is under demolition order."

Fury erupted, pointless but endearing, as if the collective will of her staff could undo a bureaucratic decree. While Sal began distributing glasses of Armagnac for a last toast, Ursula went to her inner office and retrieved the envelopes she had prepared, containing the staff's various held-back earnings. This lightened the mood somewhat, though it was a solemn group who raised their glasses together.

Ursula had no speech in mind. There was little to celebrate, only remember. "I wish to thank you all for your trust in me. I wish I could have done better by you in the end."

"It's us who owe you thanks, ma'am," Sophie said.

"To Ursula!" they cried as one, those who weren't sobbing, Rose with her head on her mother's shoulder.

Her own tears flowing, her throat nearly too tight to swallow, Ursula nodded in acknowledgement, lifted her glass to her lips. Right that the liquor should burn, to prove that life was pain, and every joy a mere interruption.

On that very thought, and despite every public entry to the house being firmly locked, the door to the salon opened, and a statuesque, dark-haired lady of evident merit strode in, her hat trailing marabou, her skirt trailing ribbons, a sullen maid in much duller clothes bringing up the rear. The assembly froze as the lady strode to the centre of the room and turned about to regard them.

Marisol, tanned like a sailor, dressed beyond even her own lofty standards. "Alors, what are you lot so miserable about?"

A Royal Pain

Intent on having a last resort before they exhausted all other options, the boys went to Charlie's directly from the hotel. Though the introductions were shamefully awkward, Izzy felt owed after Charlie's poor behaviour. Charlie tacitly agreed, himself suggesting that they might be able to manage if they pulled the bed out and slept across it rather than lengthwise.

He offered work as well, and Noel insisted they take it. That put paid to seeking new lodgings that day and every day after, as the mornings were spent sleeping in preparation for the long evenings ahead. If Charlie was still moping for his own absent love, he kept it to himself. Kept off the grog as well. The work kept them all too busy to think.

This evening's assignment was at the grandest house they'd served in yet, the place lit up like a summer's day, with a forest's worth of evergreen boughs climbing up the pillars and hanging off the walls, the sappy smell joining the miasma of sweat and perfume and naphthalene from dresses kept in storage the other eleven months of the year. Jewels gleamed on every throat and gloved wrist, though Izzy reckoned much of it was paste, many of the pieces poor copies of a certain emerald necklace being worn by a duke's daughter. Izzy and Noel had seen so many clients of theirs that pointing them out was no longer amusing. At least Noel had not been relegated to the kitchens, but the guests paid as much attention to one servant as to another, that is to say none at all.

They had formed a little crew under Charlie's direction and were presently minding the punchbowl, the glasses being taken up from the table as fast as they could fill them. Lushes, the guests were, stuffing themselves on someone else's pocketbook, competing with each other to be the grandest arsehole in the room. Charlie was in poor sorts, constantly peering about, looking the guests in the eye in a manner unbecoming a servant.

"Can you smell that?" he muttered to Izzy for the fifth time.

Izzy glanced up at the cedar branch hanging perilous inches above their heads. "I smell plenty."

"Something's burning."

Izzy took a sniff, caught the scent of wet ashes amid the greenery. "What of it?"

"I swear..." Charlie looked behind him, craning his neck.

"Going to finish that thought? Come on, you're like a cat on the coals. What's gnawing at you?"

"It smells like his cigarettes."

"Whose, your Charles?"

He glared at Izzy, jaw clenched. "I wish you'd stop calling him that."

On the other side Noel cleared his throat. Nodded towards the front of the broad salon where a fulsome woman in a heavily beaded dress was speaking with the man at the piano bench.

"Ah shit," Izzy muttered. Charlie glared at him again, but the guests were turning towards the spectacle and the vulgarity went unnoticed except by Noel, who was biting his lips and trying not to laugh. This would be their third party in a row attended by the aging soprano, who had managed every night to act surprised at being asked to sing, despite her name being written on a card on an easel by the entry. She even had a repertoire, perhaps unaware that most of the attendees would have heard her sing the very same three songs at the prior evening's event. Regardless, the toffs all applauded like trained monkeys, the singer blushing and simpering like a right professional as she took her place beside the gleaming piano.

Off she went, one hand on the piano, the other fluttering over her bosom, her whole body tensing when she reached for the high notes. Every time she went for that one, it made Izzy's teeth ache. By the end he could hum along, and had mocked up his own words to keep himself amused. Sure, he had to clench his arse to hit the high notes, but he was an untrained git and she was a blooming star. Perhaps past blooming and on to overblown. Izzy snorted, his lips clamped shut to keep from laughing aloud.

"You're going to get us sacked," Charlie hissed in his ear. "Go out to the corridor and pull yourself together."

With pleasure. Izzy sidled to the nearest door which let not onto the main area of the house but a broad corridor leading back to the clamour of the party. The cooler air was a delight after the funk of so many bodies, and with no one around he took off his gloves for a respite from their sweaty cling.

Across the corridor a door stood open a little though the room was dark. All the other doors were sealed tight, and Izzy went to shut it. Perhaps to evict whomever was in there, as he heard men talking. Not talking but arguing, the one voice full of fear, the other horribly familiar.

"I'm relying on your discretion, of course. If any rumours surface, I will of course have to attribute it to your failure to keep our little confidence. We can't have that, can we?" The first man made some whimpering reply. The other merely laughed. "Don't tempt me. You wouldn't last a week. And you can take this with you, for your insolence in suggesting it."

Izzy knew that voice. Had last heard it in a shiny new carriage while its owner had him by the throat, attempting to choke him into obedience. There was a sharp sound of skin striking skin, then a slim, weeping fellow came stumbling out, his servant's garb in disarray, his cheek stung red. He took one look at Izzy and hurried off into the bowels of the house.

Run. Run away, the other way, now, now, now... Instead Izzy stood in heart-quaking disbelief as the very spectre of all his woes emerged from the dark room, straightening the front of his trousers. On seeing Izzy the royal pain in the arse stopped, smiled revoltingly.

"So my eyes did not deceive. It was you serving that

horrid punch."

"Stay away from me," Izzy growled, trembling like a beast in a trap as it awaited the killing blow.

His awful highness laughed again, a filthy chuckle that set Izzy's teeth on edge and liquefied his innards and make his knees shake so hard he stood helpless, all but breathless as the other man approached. "I don't think so. In fact, you and I have some unfinished business, don't we?"

Mere steps away, but he paused as behind Izzy the door to the grand salon opened and let a burst of sound into the corridor.

"Pound, what are you—fucking hell!" Noel's shout of surprise was enough to break the spell, and without care or caution Izzy took off like a shot. He checked himself at the foyer, found Noel beside him, panting and wild-eyed.

"We're clearing out," Izzy hissed as they skirted the crowd, making for the servants' stairwell by the entry.

"Too right. Charlie's scarpered as well."

"Eh?"

"First he left me minding the table. Then I saw him across the room arguing with some slim bloke. Next thing I knew, they'd both gone."

"Maybe he found his Charles."

They left without asking for pay, which mollified the head butler's ire over the fact that they were leaving at all. At least Charlie had given Izzy a key to the flat. Too cold and spiritually numb to talk, they hurried home through an icy mist that was thick enough to be snow.

Charlie wasn't home and they took advantage to lay properly in the double bed. Not to fuck. Only to talk. About privilege and pain, about Charlie and his Charles, lives chosen and lives not yet lived, lives never to be. Freedom, and how impossible it was.

TWO MORE DAYS PASSED with no sign of Charlie. Izzy refused to leave the flat and Noel let him be, busying himself with looking for work. After the two days he gave up, humiliated by having gotten so soft he couldn't bring himself to do hard labour. Izzy kept his told you so's to himself.

On the third day, Noel brought home bread and ham and the newspaper, convinced he'd do better with the adverts than the jobbers' shops. They sat in bed, Noel at the head, Izzy at the foot, sandwiches and two bottles of ale on a bit of board between them, while Noel read the adverts and Izzy daydreamed about escape.

"Canada?"

"Weather's worse than here," Noel replied from behind the paper.

"The United States?"

"Not on your life. And plenty enough of that's cold as well."

"Australia? What?" he asked as Noel lowered the paper to give him a dirty look.

"I don't fancy six weeks in a rotting tub to end up on a prison farm run by red coats and the Irish."

"We don't have to get transported. We can afford proper passage. All right then, you nancy, another colony. Somewhere warm."

"Where they don't need fools like us as they've got natives to do the dirty work."

"Well, I guess it's back to selling our narrow arses to the aristocracy," Izzy said. He stretched his arms overhead cautiously, to not tip the lunch.

Noel snorted, not a laugh but at least not a moan. "I'd do it if I could do it for Ursula. We try to start trading up here, we'll get collared by some local pimp and buggered to death."

"Too right. By the stars, are we going to have to keep looking for honest work?"

Noel snorted again and rattled the newspaper at him. "What do you think I'm doing?"

He disappeared behind the paper, raising it to read below the fold. On the lower half of the front was a small boxed headline with an engraving of a face Izzy would be only too happy to never see again. "Mercy, put it down. I don't need to see that."

"Hmm?"

"RP on the bleeding front page. Like we give a rat's...hang on."

"A rat's hang on? That's a new one."

"Give me the paper, you berk."

Sucking his teeth, Noel folded the paper and tossed it at him. Izzy mouthed through the headline. Two or three lines of the article. Then he started over, read it again. "Does that say what I think it says?"

He passed it back to Noel, who ran his finger down the column "Lessee...his highness, such and such, blah de blah, has embarked on a goodwill tour of the...anti-podes? What's an antipode?"

The Antipodes. Izzy had a sudden crystal clear memory

of a yellowing map of the world, pinned up in the so-called Headmaster's Suite, back at the dear old House. "I think it means Australia. Fucking hell, Peters! That's why he was up here, to get put on a boat. The RPA's gone and got himself transported!"

HOMEWARD

THERE WAS A WAR on, and they weren't going. There was a disaster, and they'd lived through it. The end of the world had come, and they were resurrected. They spilled the lunch, leaping from the bed to dance about the flat, then embrace then kiss then fetch up against the wall, where Izzy felt compelled to prove how thoroughly relieved he was by sucking Noel inside out.

The ale was spilled, and so to toast they had to go out to the nearest public. From whence they did not move for several hours, having secured a corner table and the favour of the beleaguered barmaid with a hefty gratuity on their first round. At last, half blind with drink, mostly deaf from the clamour, they staggered out, getting halfway to the Manse before remembering where they were meant to be going. Returning the way they had come, they stopped at a different pub, or perhaps the very same, but it was snowing hard and this place was warm and loud and too crammed for any to notice if Izzy put his hand on Noel's back, if one of them looked too long at the other.

Despite Muldoon, there was no question about going back to London, no need to stay in Liverpool if the primary cause of their departure was on his way to the other end of the earth. The next day they paid out Charlie's room for a month going forward, as a kindness. Then went round the Manse and bid farewell to Mrs. Gummage, in case Ursula made contact. Thence to Lime Street and the train station and the southward journey home.

After a few hours in the stuffy, damp-smelling carriage, Noel was near crawling out of his skin. It wasn't boredom—well, it was somewhat—but more a creeping sense that they ought not to have acted so rashly in departing Liverpool. Izzy didn't know how rough things were in London, hadn't watched Ursula break down in genuine tears.

They were stopped at a village where one could see the distant hills. Snow lay over the land, the hedgerows shadowy hummocks, the roads and streams and forests dark against the dazzle, the odd trickle of smoke indicating a house. The other passengers had left their compartment and none had boarded, and Izzy slipped his hand into Noel's. He returned the pressure, held on.

"Penny for your thoughts?" Izzy said.

"Hmm?"

"You've something on your mind."

"It's nothing."

"Tell me. You looked happy there for a tick."

"Them houses, far off. I were thinking, that must be nice. Having that much quiet, that much space around. Not having to see a soul if you didn't want."

"I dunno. I'd go spare, being that much alone."

Noel bumped his shoulder against Izzy. "You'd not be alone, you twit."

Izzy coloured, rubbing his hot neck, so ready to disbelieve in his worth. "I'd not presume."

"Presume away. I been thinking about it since I saw them on the way up. That's what I wanted, to find you and take you somewhere like that, where no one could come after us and nothing we did mattered. Anyway, stupid thought." He made to unlace his fingers from Izzy's but his friend held on, and his voice shook when he spoke.

"It's not stupid at all. It's lovely."

"You got to wonder if it'll ever change. I mean, there weren't always laws, right?"

"Right. There wasn't always emancipation either."

"Exactly my point."

"And that only took, what, two, three centuries to achieve?"

They laughed, and it was good to laugh out loud, the dire facts aside. Expect nothing: that was the safest bet. Expect a life on the margins, and find a way to thrive there. On the platform, the conductor whistled for boarding. As passengers began moving along the aisle, Noel let go of Izzy's hand. What mattered was being together. That was enough.

Izzy was all for heading direct to Ursula's when they disembarked at St. Pancras late in the afternoon. Other than his fear of what they might find, Noel could come up with no reason to wait. It was raining so they caught a cab off Euston Road and were deep in Mayfair in minutes. The row where the House stood was an oddity for the borough, pinched between Spencer and the mews behind. Some of the buildings had stood for centuries as others were slapped up around, over, and on top of them, such that the only external sign of the House's age was the formidable studded door. This had been marked with chalk, which someone else had tried to smear away, but the coarse timbers held enough traces for those who knew to look.

"Ah shit," Noel muttered. They had left the cab at the end of the row and were standing under a shop awning on the other side of the street. "I didn't know she'd had to close up shop."

"Who's that standing by the door?" Izzy said. Bold as anything, a sharply dressed fellow with an ungentlemanly sneer was loitering beside, a toothpick dangling from his lips. As a better dressed man passed, he spoke, and the man startled and hurried away.

Noel's scalp prickled. "Clyde wouldn't stand for that. Which means they're not there. Or if they are, we ought not to be."

"We'll go round Owen's. She'll at least know what's what."

Off they went, Noel's fear growing with every step. Evening was falling as they came out onto Leicester Square. Owen's house was along a street of the east side, but instead of sooty brick house-fronts, there was a sturdy fence of planks that carried on to the next corner. Izzy peered through a gap between boards. Groaned, grabbing for Noel's arm like he might fall.

"This should not happen twice in a man's life."

"What are you on about?"

"It's gone."

Noel shoved him aside, pressed his eye to the gap. Saw the heaped dirt, the mounds of bricks, the carnage of a house destroyed. He pulled back as if burned. Turned to Izzy, who was down on his haunches, breathing hard, his back against the planks.

"We ought to get on." Noel put his hand out but Izzy didn't move.

"What's the bleeding point?"

"We don't know what's happened. Maybe they've got a better place round the corner."

"As if."

Noel weighed his choices. What they needed more than anything was information. If they could wring a few shillings out of getting it, so much the better. "You recall that bloke with the curly blond sideburns? That fellow that was one of Rosie's usuals?"

"What about him?"

"He came round after you'd gone. Left me his card. Offered work. In service, so I weren't jumping for joy. But he were a regular. He might know what's what."

"Huh. If nothing else, we can stand over him for twenty quid and a meal." Izzy slapped his thighs, stood up. "Come on, then. Sitting still is getting us nowhere."

He strode off and Noel hurried after. Izzy might have his moods, but they came and went like clouds before the wind. They weren't beaten yet.

The lord had a wide townhouse in Marylebone, facing a square where the chestnut trees had yet to drop their clattering canopy of dried leaves.

"This ain't too shabby for a last resort," Izzy said, peering up the well-lit street as they waited for the doorman to announce them.

"It's not a last resort. We've not even gone to see my parents yet. Or yours."

Izzy snorted in laughter. "What good will mine do? They'll want to borrow off me. Yours though, we owe a visit."

"No matter what happens here."

Before Izzy replied, the doorman returned. "His lordship is free to meet with you directly. Please, come in."

Just like that. In they went, leaving their hats and coats with the man. The interior was cool and clean-smelling and they followed another servant up the carpeted stairs to a room off the landing. His lordship stood to greet them, introduced himself as Leslie, pressed them call him by name and not title as he ushered them to a set of comfortable chairs by the fireplace.

"It's ideal you've come at this time, seeing as my wife's in Devon. Not that I have designs," Leslie added as they swapped glances. "Only I don't think she'd understand even a fraternal relationship with men in your circumstance."

"Most wives fall into that camp, to be honest," Izzy said.

"Most individuals," Noel added.

"A sad reality," Leslie sighed, as if he were the one on the outs. "I must say, at the risk of offending you both, that I consider you remarkably brave."

"Do you now?" Izzy said, settling into his chair.

"It mustn't be easy, being both disregarded and needed

desperately. And by the same people, largely."

"Your lordship is more perceptive than most men in your circumstance."

He smiled, happy to banter. "My policy is to notice much, and say little."

"If your lordship has noticed much lately, perhaps you'll do us the favour of telling us a little."

"I assume you mean your place of employment. I can't speak to what's happened, but they closed, oh, four days ago? Anyone who held credit received a reimbursement in the post. That was an unpleasant conversation, I must say. I ended up giving it straight to my wife. Which is why she's in Dover. At her mother's. With the children."

"And you're all on your lonesome," Izzy prompted.

"I am, and with nowhere to go. The mood at my club's dire. Everyone's had the wind put up them by this espionage imbroglio."

"Espionage?" Noel said. Was there no end to the madness swirling around them?

"Heavens, you have missed a lot," Leslie went on, stretching his legs towards the cheery fire. "I'm well out of it, but there's been dreadful trouble over some supposed ring of foreign spies, milking fools of my ilk out of their ministerial secrets. It's given the police justification for putting a stop to all manner of illicit trades. The, ah, skin trade among them."

"Do you suppose Ursula's been arrested?" Noel asked, embarrassed by the tremor in his voice.

"You likely can find out," Leslie said. "Go to the nearest police station and—"

"No thanks. Unless your lordship's offering to do the

leg work yourself."

"I may be able to assist, though we'd have to wait until tomorrow. Unless you feel she's in immediate danger."

Of course she was. They all were. It hardly mattered if the royal pain was out of the way, if everything else was a disaster. But surely Ursula's paid-off coppers would keep her out of the worst of it. Wouldn't they?

Izzy and Lord Leslie were making plans for tomorrow, but the words passed Noel's ears like the clatter of leaves in the wind. The night to come concerned him more, the hours before they could return to hear what his lordship had found out. They didn't even know the prick's last name, and here was Izzy dishing out every detail of their miserable lives to a man who could be a nose himself, for the Yard or for those foreign spies.

Noel hissed to Izzy, who leaned near. "We ought to get on."

"Why?"

"We've taken more than enough of his lordship's time."

"By no means," the fellow said. "You've preserved me from a very dull evening. In fact, you're welcome to stay a little longer. I'd be glad of the conversation."

"Up to you," Izzy said quietly to Noel. "I'm happy either way."

"Might his lordship excuse us for a moment?" Noel said carefully, but the man smiled and stood up.

"Perhaps I'll see what might be had for dinner."

As he closed the door behind him Izzy sat back and scratched his balls. "I've been waiting this whole time for that," he groaned. "How do they maintain decorum on the day to day?"

"By getting you and me to whip 'em into shape night to night."

"You reckon that's what he's after?"

"Why wouldn't it be? Empty house, two desperate skin traders." Restless, regretting more by the minute his suggestion to come here, Noel got up, stalked to the curtained window. There was nothing to see but the night, the tossing trees concealing the houses across the way, the sky a sooty blanket of clouds. Snow was due, as if it had followed them southward. They had nowhere else to go.

AUNTIE

HE KNEW NOEL'S RELUCTANCE, having felt it so often himself. Some choices were barely choices, but they weren't beat yet, not by any means. He got up and joined Noel at the window. His friend was lost in thought and didn't stir when Izzy put his arm around his waist.

"I'll run out of pennies at this rate."

"Hmm?" Noel blinked like he was waking.

"For your thoughts."

He swallowed, made to speak, nearly didn't, made himself go on, though his gaze was on the darkened sky. "Are we awful?"

"If awful means won't give up, won't back down, won't regret what I do to keep my skin intact, then yes. That's me to a T."

"But can a man be good when he does wrong?"

"What do we do that's wrong?"

Noel eyed him with that hard glare that made him resemble his father. "Are you serious?"

"Laws is laws. Made by man. Ten minutes listening to them Eton lads blather about the Greeks ought to have put paid to any notion that sodomy uncivilizes a fellow."

"That's the past."

"And so will all this be someday. Until then I ain't going to obey the laws of men who can buy their way free of the consequences they'd visit on me. I'm having my life. And that means you, my love."

Noel's cheeks flushed. "Say that again."

"My love. My darling. My everything."

Shaking, Noel bowed his head, and Izzy drew him closer. Touched his dear face, kissed his cheek. The touch brought him alive, and he clutched Izzy to him, returned his kisses with full passion. Damn the world, its laws and its lies. This was their world, this unstoppable, unspeakable love.

The snow had started in earnest, and when Leslie returned he insisted they stay overnight. After an awkward but enjoyable bachelor's meal—sausages, gherkins, vodka on ice—they retired for the evening, despite the quantity of wistful looks his lordship cast in their direction. Rather than sending them to bunk with the staff, he surprised them by granting them use of an upstairs bedroom. It was a very nice room, nicer even than that Mersey hotel, Izzy's toes sinking into the dove-grey carpet with each step.

Noel had undressed quickly as was his way and was already under the covers. "Saints above..." he sighed as he sank back into the mound of pillows. "If I were a lord, I swear I'd never get up."

"Run your empire from your bed?" Izzy said as he hung his trousers over a nearby chair.

"You'd like that, wouldn't you?" Noel replied, his hand moving suggestively under the blanket.

Izzy only smiled, too conscious of Leslie, alone in his room down the corridor. Not the idea that he'd come peeping, but simply that the man was alone. Poverty was a hell, but such lonesome luxury was its own sort of death. Even luxury could be cold on a cold enough night, and he shivered as he slipped between the sleek sheets. Noel reached for him and he went into his arms.

Sanctuary: in the warmth of Noel's body, the strength of his embrace, the rhythm of his blessed heart, beating in time with Izzy's as he lay with his head cradled on Noel's shoulder.

"Thank you for coming to find me," he murmured, though in his mind he shouted it to the heavens.

Noel's arm tightened around him. "Thank God that I could," he replied thickly.

"Balls to God." Izzy raised his head to look Noel in the eye. "He ain't done for me half of what you have. He's the prick what made all the rest happen. You're the one who saved me."

They kissed, but only that, the room too vast, the night too cold, the day too strange to spark a hotter desire. To kiss was enough, was everything, Noel's love a prize beyond measure, a miracle. Sanctuary.

NOEL WOKE IN THE grey dawn, or so he thought by the faint gleam at the edge of the drapes. Pushing one aside, he was blinded by the dazzle of full day.

"D'you mind?" Izzy groaned. He pulled his pillow around his ears and burrowed under the covers again.

"We ought to get going."

"Why?" came the muffled reply. "Got nowhere to go, nothing to do when we get there."

"I've got to see my folks. They likely think I'm dead." It was an indignity to let them believe so. Izzy relented, got up, got dressed. This room had bathing facilities though not as grand as those in his lordship's suite, and they were much refreshed by the time they made their way downstairs. Their hats and coats were waiting on a stand by the front door. That seemed a move too bold, and they went through to the rear of the house, where a startled maid showed them out by the servants' door. The garden path had been swept of snow but the streets were ankle deep and their feet were soon damp once more.

"That was luck, having him put us up," Izzy said, kicking slush with every step.

"Yeah, but now what?"

"Let's go by Auntie's laundry. She's always got the goss. Plus we can have her deal with this." He hefted the Gladstone bag, the contents of which were starting to reek. "Then to your folks for dinner. Why are you laughing?"

"I'm not used to you being so practical."

"It's my duty. Managing the household for my husband."

"Your jobless, homeless tart of a husband, you mean."

Izzy winked up at him. "Exactly. You need caring for. Bleeding useless on your own."

"Kiss my arse."

"Make me. But maybe not in public. People will talk."

Griping joyfully, feeling flush, they took a cab all the way out to the bridge then walked across. The snow had fallen more thickly here, but the bridge was much travelled and was mainly clear. Partway they stopped, looking downriver towards the snow-capped city, from which rose a grey haze from a hundred thousand chimneys.

"Wouldn't hardly know from up here how grimy it is down there," Noel mused.

"It's to keep us thinking it's better on the other side. Tell you what though, much more bad news and I'll be ready to throw in the towel on this cursed city, find us one of them little cottages of yours in the middle of nowhere."

"I'd keep us fed," Noel said as they carried on. "We'll get some birds for eggs. A pig or two."

"What on earth would we do with a pig?"

"Eat it."

"Fair enough."

It was a fine winter's day, and everywhere in the snow were tracks from children's feet and sledge runners. The Peters family had done for the day at the garden and no one was about, so the boys carried on towards the clutch of houses and businesses that once upon a time had been a village and was soon to be just another borough of the city that never stopped spreading.

Knowing they were likely to be all day at Noel's parents', they went directly to the laundry. It at least was unchanged, the same roiling cloud of steam and smoke above, the same sweaty conditions inside the low stone building, which word had it once had been a dairy when a Roman villa had stood on the hillside.

Rose's aunt owned the laundry. A thick-set woman with

the burnished face, bowed back, and chafed hands of her profession, she'd known Noel all his life, and insisted that he bend down so she could pinch his cheek.

"It does me such good to see you," she sighed. "I weren't expecting you back from France so soon."

"Things have changed, Auntie, and—"

"Hang on," Izzy said, grabbing for Noel's sleeve. "Auntie, did you say France?"

On the Beach

Through the years of their acquaintance, Ursula had heard enough stories of Marisol's manic, profligate, possibly incestuous family to expect nearly anything from the woman. She had therefore been only mildly surprised to learn that Marisol had inherited a manor in the French countryside, some five miles from Calais on a glorious sweep of golden beach facing the Dover coast.

On her initial visit, Marisol's solicitor had only been able to show her the exterior of the house. The interior turned out to be close to a ruin, having been dwelt in by all manner of itinerants, not to mention wildlife, in the two decades it had been neglected by her uncle, who had been penned up until his death in an elite asylum in Marseilles for having shot his wife, his horse, and then himself—this last not lethally—under exceedingly dubious circumstances Ursula had begged Marisol not to relate.

Along with the grand stuccoed house had come a considerable endowment, which Marisol was more than willing to spend in the name of freedom. The staff had been ready to supplement with whatever they had to offer, and within a day a small army of eager craftsmen was busily retiling the roof, repointing the walls, and carting endless barrow-loads of debris to the rubbish pit.

Not that the women had been idle. For one thing, the contents of the House of Lords had been packed in such haste that in every trunk and suitcase was a jumble of dresses and rugs and corsets and floggers, all in need of sorting. After a solid week's work, most of the rooms had been cleared and a good number of the bedchambers were habitable. Ursula had called a holiday, and a few brave souls had set off for Calais, easily reached by walking along the beach. Enough farms lay about that one could almost always find a ride home on the back of a wagon.

Though Christmas was nearly upon them, the weather was fairer than in Britain, the wind seeming to push away the clouds before they could ever settle. The air was tremendous, bringing Ursula back to her youth at the institute, the garden of which had overlooked the sea. The waves here were kinder, not smashing into the dark cliffs of a fjord but rolling onto pale sand which would be a holiday-maker's dream when the weather turned.

It was this on which her hopes hung, that the springtime would bring an influx of wealthy Britons who might wish to visit a bawdy house in a nation with far laxer indecency laws. Five miles from Calais could not be any more convenient for a gentleman who wished to obtain all the delights of Paris without having to travel so far. Time would tell, and for now it was enough that they were safe.

If she only knew what her boys were doing. She would

never have referred to them as such to their faces, but she felt protective of Noel and Ezekiel, in way she did not with the women. How strange, how utterly strange and sad, that mothering should always come at such a cost. That love could hurt so much and so continuously. And that one kept on loving, regardless.

Clyde had brought a chair to the shore for her, and she watched Brigid, Noreen, and Rose sport about on the sand like children freed after a long school day, their skirts rucked up, hair loose on the breeze. Brigid and Rose were gathering driftwood for an evening fire, Noreen pointing out choice pieces from her vantage on a tumble of rocks.

"I can still see the others, I think," she called, shielding her eyes as she gazed up the strand. "Or is that someone else? Cor, Ursula, you might already have custom."

"What do you mean, dear?"

"I can see Annie and them, up ahead. They're with some men. Looks like someone they know."

"How can you tell?" Brigid said, squinting towards Calais as if her poor eyes could reach so far when she sometimes couldn't recognize a person from the far end of a room.

"They're embracing. Jumping around like mad. One of 'em is...holy Mother, is that Noelly?"

"Help me up," Ursula said. Rose helped her from the low canvas chair and they joined the others at the rocks. Perhaps a mile away along the shore, one could see the bright specks of three women's dresses and two black-clad forms, dancing about.

"Are you well, ma'am?" Brigid said, taking Ursula's elbow. "You want to sit down, you're all pale."

"Take me to them."

"Ma'am?"

"I'll go mad from waiting. Help me."

At high tide they would have had to wade through the high grass in the meadow. As it was, Ursula leaned heavily on Brigid's arm as they crossed the flat outcropping of black rocks that set apart this section of the sandy shore from the long sweep of beach that led to Calais.

The other group had started their way, and for far too long they neared each other without seeming to get any closer. Then the two lanky black figures broke from the others, came running. Ursula would have run if she could, and then Rose was on her other side, and she and Brigid took her firmly under the arms and it was if Ursula flew the last few hundred yards, her feet hardly touching the ground.

THEY HAD SPENT THE entirety of the ferry passage from Dover convinced that they would be refused entry to France. Apparently if one had the means to purchase a ticket, one was deemed too wealthy to be troublesome, for they were summarily passed along and let loose.

By Auntie's word, the 'fine house' of Marisol's was only a few miles from town, directly along the beach. An hour later, their shoes full of damp sand, their eyes parched by the constant wind off the sea, Noel had begun to regret their haste, for they hadn't passed a building larger than a cowshed. Far down the beach were figures, and they decided to carry on. The figures grew larger, until it was clear they were women, walking in their direction.

"That's some fancy clothing for farmers' wives," Izzy muttered, squinting at the brightly dressed women.

"Holiday makers?"

"It's the middle of winter."

"You don't think it's...Rose?" Because he'd known her for so long. Because he had loved her as a child, loved her now as a friend. Because she was Rosie, and once upon a time he'd wished her to be his Rosie, until this scrawny brat beside him had got into his heart. Because of this, Noel would have known Rose Owen anywhere, and when he shouted her name she waved in answer.

Unfettered jubilation reigned. Every familiar face was a blessed relief, another life not lost to the disaster. When at last they reached her, Ursula wept, embraced them both, could not stop touching them, and he and Izzy walked her up to the house between them, triumphant.

Never mind that the house was hardly a triumph. More like half a ruin, but houses could be mended, and there was Clyde, chopping firewood. There in the cavernous kitchen, dear Mrs. Owen, rolling pastry dough; Marisol loafing against the table, sneaking pieces of fruit meant for the pie; Sal at the hob, stirring something delicious-smelling. The women of the House who hadn't come over were safe, gone to ground with their families, cleared out of London entirely.

There were no beds free, the women already sharing. There was however the old caretaker's cottage. "I thought I might keep it for myself, but I found it almost too peaceful," Ursula said, her swaying lantern illuminating the plumes of their breath in the cold air as she led them to the little hut that evening, after many hours of laughing and eating and drinking and crying and overcoming their disbelief that they had come through the storm. "You might prefer the privacy however."

"Not a soul for miles, eh?" Izzy asked. In the dark, his hand found Noel's, held on.

"A few farms, but not in, er, audible distance, if that's what you're inquiring, Mr. Pound."

"I thought I'd never get to hear you say that again, ma'am. It does a body good." He was grinning, teeth catching the light, his hand shaking. Or was that Noel himself, beset with impossible happiness, terrified that this was merely some daydream he was having on the train northward, that none of the goodness had happened. This much joy couldn't be within their reach.

Ursula unlocked the door then gave Noel the heavy key. "Don't lose this. We haven't another." Izzy inhaled sharply, as if she'd said something shocking, but didn't speak as Ursula gave him the lantern. "I don't expect you'll need me to come in," she said. "And don't feel you need to get up tomorrow at any particular time. It's rather a holiday atmosphere around here."

"Yes, ma'am," Noel said, for Izzy was trembling too hard. Ursula was smiling, such a rarity, but then none of them had ever been so free.

"I'll bid you good night. Mr. Pound, Mr. Peters," she said, tipping her head to each, leaving them to enter the cottage together.

It was perfectly enough. A single room larger than any they'd had, with a high roof of beams and thatch. A stone sink, a square table, two chairs. A ladder to reach a loft where one might keep things. And below this, a bed, more than large enough, given how they'd made do elsewhere. Noel locked the door, then hung the key on a nail hammered into the frame for doubtless this purpose.

"Everything but the chickens and pigs," Izzy said hoarsely, placing the lantern on the table.

"And all we had to do was renounce the land of our birth."

Izzy laughed, and deep in Noel something came undone, a barrier between his heart and mind, as if he hadn't dared believe in this man's love, in case it was lost to him. And yet here it was. Here he was, and though their lives had changed, through everything that might come, they would face it together.

"Between you and Mother England?" Izzy said with that dear old crooked grin as he pulled off his coat and threw it aside. "That bitch never stood a chance. Now get over here and make me holler till they hear us in Calais."

Thanks for reading.
I'd love it if you took a moment to leave a review!

ACKNOWLEDGMENTS

NONE OF THIS WOULD be possible without my wonderfully supportive and endlessly helpful husband Derek, who understands what it means when I'm behind that blue curtain and cannot be disturbed.

Special thanks to Britt Hanowell of Boundless Words, whose input on the sequel guided the completion of this book as well.

I also want to mention the incredible support I and so many other authors get from Craig Martelle and the whole fifty-thousand-odd members of the 20 Books to 50k© crew. This group is my lode-stone, my guiding light, my reason for being able to sit down at the keyboard every day and write another story. Look them up if you want to know all there is about bringing your story to the world.

And thanks to you, for reading all the way to the end!

OTHER *LONDON HUSTLE* BOOKS

THE OLD RAZZLE DAZZLE

An "R-rated Queer historical Hallmark movie" (Britt Hanowell, Boundless Words) about the astonishing rise (and almost fall) of two very different heroes, set against the backdrop of theatre life in London's West End at the dawn of a new century.
www.willforrest.com/london-hustle/

BACKSTAGE PASS

Made to Measure – For His Eyes Only
A Proper Homecoming – Sleeping Beauty
Four tales of unabashed eroticism. Dressed up, dressed down, in costume or stripped bare, Izzy never fails to satisfy Noel's every dark desire. For two unrepentant sinners, theirs is a match made in heaven.
FREE DOWNLOAD AT:
www.books.willforrest.com/BackstagePassCollection

ALSO BY WILL FORREST

AN INCONVENIENT EARL
THE UNTAMED HEART
HOW TO RESCUE A BARONESS
A PEARL FOR AN EARL
A LOVE UNBROKEN

SERIES & COLLECTIONS

LONDON HUSTLE
HOLLOWOOD FALLS
THE JAIME SKYE CHRONICLES
THE LIBERTINES
SOCIETY WIVES

COMING IN 2024

AUTHOR, AUTHOR
STARMAN
Join the Readers Club for updates & free books: willforr
est.com/newsletter/

About the Author

AUTHOR, BLOGGER, AND GENERAL nuisance Will Forrest writes unusual (and usually queer) Historical and Paranormal Romances with a dash of mischief and mayhem, and grew up on a steady diet of Douglas Adams and 'Sweet Valley High.'

Will has a diploma of fashion design, a degree in social theory, and a bad habit of changing careers, life goals, and continents. Currently Will lives in a very warm part of Canada with three lovely humans and a succession of martyred houseplants.

www.willforrest.com

Will overshares on Instagram and more sedately on Facebook as WillForrestTheWriter
Join Will's Readers Club for free books, great deals, and exclusive content, and occasionally recipes
www.willforrest.com/newsletter/
or scan the link!